# Praise for Vivian Arend's
## *Black Gold*

"The intense sexual encounters between Gem and Shaun, paired with the thickness in the air of an always lingering fight, are sure to keep the pages turning... Arend's latest is a steamy weekend escape from reality."

~ *Library Journal*

"Vivian Arend does a wonderful job of building the atmosphere and the other characters in this story so that readers will be sucked into the world and looking forward to the rest of the books in the series."

~ *The Romance Studio*

"*Black Gold* is a gem of a paranormal story. The werewolves are heart-stopping and the love between mates is strong. Vivian Arend paints a picture of pain and love no one could deny... a superb vehicle that showcases the amazing writing talent of Vivian Arend."

~ *Coffee Time Romance*

"Steamy and sweet complete with a whole host of colourful side characters and enough sub-plots to get your teeth into. A fab read!"

~ *Scorching Book Reviews*

# Look for these titles by
## *Vivian Arend*

## *Now Available:*

# Black Gold

*Vivian Arend*

SAMHAIN
PUBLISHING

Samhain Publishing, Ltd.
11821 Mason Montgomery Road, 4B
Cincinnati, OH 45249
www.samhainpublishing.com

Black Gold
Copyright © 2012 by Vivian Arend
Print ISBN: 978-1-60928-709-2
Digital ISBN: 978-1-60928-525-8

Editing by Anne Scott
Cover by Angela Waters

First Samhain Publishing, Ltd. electronic publication: September 2011
First Samhain Publishing, Ltd. print publication: August 2012

# Dedication

Bree and Donna—you talked me through this one. Thanks for your support, understanding and general kick-assedness. So glad we get to share this crazy journey.

Anne. The wolfie adventure continues/starts anew. From that first email to now, you've proved again and again you are more than my editor. Thank you for the lessons, hugs, kicks in the butt. You rock.

# Part One

There's a race of men that don't fit in,
A race that can't stay still;
So they break the hearts of kith and kin,
And they roam the world at will.
They range the field and they roam the flood,
And they climb the mountain's crest;
Theirs is the curse of the gypsy blood,
And they don't know how to rest.

*"The Men That Don't Fit In"—Robert Service*

# Chapter One

"Excuse me, ladies."

Shaun ducked in front of a table of laughing women and caught the flying beer mug in mid-air before it could slam into the center of their party. Unfortunately, there was no time to respond with more than a wink to their admiring feminine responses. He twirled to grab the nearest bear shifter by the scruff of the neck, hauled him away from the innocent bystanders and thumped him face-first into the rustic wood-paneled wall. Another glass shattered inches to Shaun's right, and he sighed.

Bloody den buddies. Wolves might drive him crazy, but after a few too many drinks bears were even worse. Should have cut them off hours ago and sent them all packing.

"Let me know if you need a hand," Evan called from behind the bar, amusement tingeing his voice.

"Fuck off," Shaun tossed back easily. Just what he needed—an Alpha with an attitude. *Not.*

Evan laughed as he reached over the counter and nabbed the nearest two troublemakers by the hair. He knocked their heads together and grinned with satisfaction as the shifters tumbled to the floor.

Shaun pulled his current object of attention off the wall a foot or so, examined the man's eyes carefully, then slammed him back harder than the time before. The bear shifter went limp and puddled downward without a sound. Shaun turned to the remaining crew of shaggy-headed rabble-rousers currently making Tuesday afternoon in Whitehorse a little too exciting for the locals.

Of course, at this time of day the only occupants of the Moonshine Pub were shifters, and for the most part, they weren't as picky about how wild the party got.

"Hey, watch it, buddy. You're shaking the dartboard."

Shaun flipped the visiting wolves the finger. Figured they'd sit and observe the chaos instead of offering to help. This wasn't their territory, so he couldn't blame them for staying out of it. And with Whitehorse in the strange position of having two packs sharing territory—sometimes not getting mixed up in local werewolf politics was the safest way to keep your fur intact.

He took a swift survey of the bar, noting only four grizzly shifters remained standing. Well, three standing, one swaying violently as he attempted to chug the remaining half pint of beer in his mug and keep an eye on Shaun.

Talk about not taking matters seriously. For some reason the big brute's lack of concentration pissed Shaun off. He shook his hands at the man like an irate Italian. "Hey, you. Put the glass down and let's see some effort here. *Sheesh*, what kind of barroom brawl is this?"

His opponents exchanged glances, and Shaun cracked his knuckles in anticipation. Finally he'd get to inflict a little bodily damage. Not that he had anything against bears personally—it had simply been too long since he'd let off some steam.

One bear rushed him. Shaun sidestepped, turning with his elbow raised high and hard, connecting with a satisfying *thunk* to the idiot's head. The second swung at him as the third lunged forward. Shaun seized the ham-sized fist on his right as it approached, pulled the man off balance and into the direct line of the dive-bombing attack of his buddy. The two connected with grunts of pain, tangling together to land in a twisted mess on the floor.

Too damn easy. Shaun shook his head in disgust and stepped over their prone bodies before they could scramble to their feet. A quick one-two kick to each of their stomachs ensured that the only thing they would be concentrating on for the next few minutes was their next breath.

"I don't know, Evan. Maybe you should reconsider the whole public-bar idea. I mean..." The grizzly shifter sneaking up on Shaun was reflected in the mirror behind the counter. Shaun waited one more second then raised his clenched fist as if he were doing a strongman muscle pose. The back of his hand connected with the man's face, and the bear teetered on shaky legs, the stars he must be seeing almost visible in the air.

*Shit, that one hurt.* Shaun shook out his fingers and concentrated. Where was he? Oh, right.

"What if you made the place private? This dealing with tourists is bullshit."

Evan rinsed a glass. "It's the tourists passing through who make life interesting. Winter season gets too quiet and cozy with only locals dropping in."

That was true enough. Watching water freeze was right up there on the list of entertaining things to do during December in the Yukon, and didn't keep the blood stirring. Still...

"I didn't think returning to the Takhini pack would involve so much fighting."

"Are you serious? Shaun, what the hell else do you know that is so universally acceptable amongst every wolf pack? Huh?"

11

Shaun shrugged. Yeah, pack hierarchy games came with the territory. "Not every pack spends *all* their time jostling for position."

Evan paused in the middle of wiping the counter. "It's not a bad source of entertainment." He twirled, slamming a fist between the eyes of the grizzly standing behind him with a chair lifted in his hands. The huge man fell like a tree trunk, chair crashing to the floor. Shaun rolled his eyes as Evan did a celebratory dance behind the bar.

His Alpha completed his gyrating and tilted his head toward the unconscious shifter. "You want to clean that up, or should I call the cops?"

Shaun grabbed his beer from where he'd hidden it and snuck a swig. "Nah, don't bother the RCMP. They're busy enough with spring fever hitting everyone in town. I'll pour the bears into a cab and get them dumped in the bush."

"Shaun..."

"Fine, fine. I'll send them to their hotel. Damn, you're no fun at all." Shaun winked at his Alpha. There was no doubt Evan was the strongest wolf in the area, but the dude was nuttier than a fruitcake at times. Newcomers didn't seem to understand why the Takhini pack put up with such an oddball for a leader, but even in the short time Shaun had been back in Whitehorse, he'd come to appreciate Evan's style. The man didn't give a damn about being the most powerful. He simply was, no gesturing, no chest beating.

Evan's sense of the ridiculous appealed to Shaun in a thumb-your-nose-at-authority kind of way.

Shaun levered one of the groaning bodies upright off the floor. "Okay, big guy. Time to pay the bills and take your little party elsewhere."

The shifter made a pathetic attempt to bat away Shaun's

hands. "Piss off."

"Tsk, tsk, that's not how to talk to the guy who's still deciding if you go in a cab or the river."

By the time Shaun had poured the bears into cabs, he was ready for another drink. Just one last body to deal with. He grabbed the dead weight of the biggest guy by the ankles and tugged, attempting to slide him over the rough wooden boards of the bar toward the door. It was after five, and action around the place had increased in a slow trickle. More of the pack wandered in. Servers rushed in, carrying orders of wings and plates of appetizers. The live band tuned up, the drummer beating out a heavy pulse that throbbed below the murmuring voices. The evening was warm enough Evan had cracked open the windows, and an early June breeze fluttered in carrying the smell of spring and the promise of a great outdoor adventure season.

*Yada, yada, yada.* Shaun yanked harder on his burden, managing to drag the heavy weight a measly two inches. Only a couple days left before his temporary break in bookings was over and he'd be flying tourists again. This hanging-out-with-the-pack thing wasn't as bad as he had expected.

It was worse.

"You know, you could ask for help." Evan motioned toward the pack members crowding the pub.

"When pigs fly."

Evan laughed out loud, pausing to call a few of the guys from their beers. The nearest three leapt to their feet in response. They grabbed the griz under the arms and manhandled him out the door.

Shaun slid back onto his barstool. "Is there nothing I can say that will piss you off?"

Evan considered for a minute. He shook his head as he

reached under the bar and brought up a dusty bottle of liquor, lowering the pale blue decanter to the counter with reverence. "See, I understand where you're coming from. You want me to get mad and tell you to take a hike. Therefore, the most fun I can have is to force you to stick around until you get your head out of your ass."

He grabbed two glasses and motioned to one of the pack who took over serving. "Come on, we're going to my office."

*Fuck.* This kind of summons was as bad as getting called to the principal's. "Ah, gee thanks, Evan, but I should get home. I've got a big flight planned in a couple days. I need to get my beauty sleep. There's this really good movie on APN."

"You forgot the excuse about needing to wash your hair." Evan pushed open the solid wood door leading to his office and gestured Shaun in first. "Forget it. I'm not ordering you around, but if you know what's good for you, you'll get your butt in there."

Landing in Whitehorse was unadventurous, just like Gemmita had promised her father at least a dozen times it would be. The place was even smaller than she'd calculated when she'd insisted he had no need to worry, or provide an escort. The teeny airport had one luggage carousel, and the teeming crowd of greeters meeting the plane numbered twenty at the most. So far, her trip had been perfect. A chance for her to spread her wings and prove she had more going for her than the family name.

Two wolves loitered by the coffee shop. Considering how well wolves aged, she figured they must be somewhere between twenty and fifty years old. Black hair and eyes, smoky-coloured skin. Not as dark as hers, but not white either. They waggled their brows in her direction, but Gem pointedly ignored them, at least until they approached, interest gleaming in their eyes.

"Hello, sweets. You need a ride?"

She examined the mural on the wall behind the luggage carousel as if it were a Picasso, figuring silence was the best response.

The second wolf stepped to the right, neatly caging her between them before she could protest. They weren't crowding her or looming over her, or anything that seemed like an attempt to freak her out. They were just being, well, wolves.

"If you have someone coming to greet you, they're late. We'll make sure you get where you want to go."

Well, shoot. Here she hoped she'd be able to avoid the whole hierarchy and sniffing-for-importance obsession. Guess it didn't matter if you were in the Deep South or the Far North.

It was a public place with humans near at hand, so she wasn't afraid. Not really—or not enough for her to order them to stand down. In fact, this was a perfect time for her to test-drive her new "assume control of her own life" skills and get them to listen without playing on her family background.

She lifted her chin resolutely. "Thank you, boys, but I'll hail a cab and find my own way. Understand?"

Along with her words she let the tiniest touch of her power sneak out—enough to prove she wasn't a weak wolf. That bit of power was all her own, nothing to do with her name or money. The sensation thrilled her as always, the rare moments she used that other side of herself, and she fully expected both her annoyances to stage a rapid retreat.

Their response was not as respectful as the average wolf back home. In fact, they barely moved, the older of the two raising one brow as if he was more interested than before. A momentary flash of dismay shot through her, and she stomped her reaction into submission before her frustration showed.

Personal pep-talk time.

*Press forward, Gem, you can do this. Don't wait for someone to rescue you.*

She reached for her bag, but the wolf on her left snatched it up first. With all the humans around, she didn't want to make a loud scene, instead stepping forward to block his path. "Do you have a hearing problem?"

He smiled, his teeth flashing white against his skin. "Nah. You said you needed a cab." The Bobbsey Twins whipped out matching caps and slapped them on their heads. Solid black graphics declared *Whitehorse Wolves Transport*, accompanied by the imprint of a wolf in hot pursuit of a terrified horse, and she sniffed to refrain from smiling.

Her second suitcase cruised past on the carousel, and she resigned herself to accepting their help. If they stepped out of line, she had more strength she could whammy them with. "Fine. One of you grab that blue bag as well. I'm staying at the Moonshine Inn."

"Then that's where we'll take you." The younger wolf offered his elbow and Gem adjusted her thinking. Maybe they weren't all roughnecks and lowbrow here in the north. She got to embrace that charitable thought for a full minute before he helped her into the cab and managed to pinch her butt in the process. He waited until his buddy got behind the wheel, then waved at the retreating cab like a little girl, fingers fluttering innocently as they left him behind in the parking area.

Wolves. She peeked in the mirror and checked her lipstick.

"You in town for long?" The name posted on the cabby's ID was David.

"Just passing through. I'm heading to the northern part of the territory to do some research, and my pilot is supposed to meet me here."

He whistled softly. "Research, hey? What's your specialty? Let me guess—botany. I heard they were doing a study on the microsomes of the aspidiaceae ferns. Sounded fascinating."

The steep incline of the road as they descended into the river valley was forgotten as she again fine-tuned her attitude. A cabbie wolf who knew botany? Gem's enthusiasm burst out unchecked. "I'm conducting an environmental assessment on the Porcupine Caribou herd birthing grounds. With the oil and gas development, it's of vital importance to maintain up-to-date statistics on any changes."

"Really? That's fabulous as well." He grinned at her, the leer fading, replaced with a touch of something else.

Was he...? Was that...? My goodness, he was *laughing* at her.

Gem stiffened her spine. She wasn't used to being made fun of to her face. In fact, no one in her pack would dream of doing anything but treat her with respect in public. She stifled a sigh. If only being shown respect meant they actually respected her. That was part of the point of this journey—to prove she could stand on her own without Daddy interfering.

There was no reason for her to be impolite in return. "You're well educated for a cab driver."

He shrugged, slowing for a crosswalk. "People come north for many reasons. When a soul gets tired of the big city and the whole rat race, the Yukon offers a different pace of life."

Gem considered his words as she watched the city drift past her window. A bookstore, tiny eclectic coffee shops, intricate carved wooden signs offering native crafts and moccasins. None of the buildings were over two stories high, and many of them sported false fronts, their doors opening onto an elaborate boardwalk that ran the length of Main Street. The restoration of Whitehorse into a gold rush settlement gave her glimpses of the rough town she'd been warned, repeatedly, would be too much for her to handle. Too primitive and coarse.

Yet, there was more to a place than just its buildings. Maybe a different pace of life was a good thing? She was sure her father hadn't considered that possibility.

"So you came north—and now you drive a cab for a living?"

David chuckled. "No, I drive a cab because I like to talk to people. I don't need the money, but our Alpha insists everyone work. Being busy is the only way to keep your average wolf out of trouble."

Blast, with everything else she had to accomplish before hopping on the plane, that important detail had slipped her agenda. She was in another pack's territory. "I suppose I should stop in and say hello, shouldn't I?"

"That's where I was taking you, to our Alpha, whether you wanted me to or not." They paused at an intersection before he turned into the hotel entrance. "I get heads-up of all official visitors. If they're short-termers, Evan lets them pass without a hassle since they've gone through the decency of contacting him. You weren't on the list."

Fudge. "I'm only in town for a few days…"

He clicked his tongue, and Gem felt about twelve years old at the disapproval clear in his reproachful tone. "There's no excuse for poor manners, now, is there?"

David pulled up to the front of the hotel. She fidgeted the entire time as she waited for him to come around and open her door. Oh dear, this was not a good start to her Yukon excursion. "I really did intend to make my presence known."

"I'm sure you did. No harm done. Now let's get you settled."

He patted her hand kindly, and a sudden wave of

homesickness flooded her system. His patience reminded her of her father, even more so when he waved off her credit card. "Complimentary shuttle service, since you're staying at the pack hotel."

The cab ride had only taken ten minutes, airport to hotel, but the freebie was unexpected. "The pack? I didn't know that."

David lifted her bags and nodded toward the front doors. "The Takhini pack owns the hotel, and Evan owns the bar."

"Your Alpha?"

"Yup." He shook her cases. "We can drop these at the registration desk, then I'll take you to see him."

The double doors slid open with a soft sigh, and Gem glanced around with curiosity as they entered. The welcoming foyer was as tidy as any resort she'd visited with her father down south. Swarms of plants filled the perimeter of the reception area, accompanied by the flash of modern chrome and leather.

"No fake boardwalks or gold rush decorating?"

David snorted. "The bar is more rustic, but no. Visitors get enough history walking downtown. We decided to make the place a bit of a refuge from the turn-of-the-century overload you can get otherwise."

Smart move. She certainly felt more comfortable in this setting than if there had been rough-hewn boards or spittoons on the floor.

Not that she knew up close and in person what a spittoon looked like.

"Caroline, can you get our new arrival fixed up?" David placed her bags by the desk. The very efficient blonde human behind the counter gave him a wink before taking Gem through the check-in process. She seemed unconcerned she was surrounded by werewolves.

Gem watched Caroline with unashamed interest. At home, everyone was a wolf—from her extended family down to the servants in the familial mansion. When it came right down to it, she hadn't been close to that many humans. Taking another glance at the receptionist, Gem sized her up. Pretty creature. Smelled faintly like a wolf, probably because she was around them so often. Decent clothing, although with her blonde hair and lighter skin—Gem jerked upright. Oh shoot, this train of thought wasn't acceptable. She was being a snob. Just because Whitehorse was above the sixtieth parallel didn't mean all the residents were uncultured rednecks.

If she was tired of being unfairly judged, she'd better not do it herself.

"Is Evan working?" David asked, leaning on the counter.

Caroline glanced at a monitor. "He's not serving, and I see a 'do not disturb' notification on his office line. Do you want me to send through a message that you need to see him?"

David put the question to Gem. "You want to wait in the bar for a few minutes?"

"Could I go to my room first?" From traveling all day to heading straight to see an Alpha? One whom she might have inadvertently upset by breaking protocol? No way. She needed to be fresh and dressed for success, not wearing wrinkled and travel-worn clothes.

"Sure. I'll give you some time. We can have a drink until Evan is free. Caroline, send him a note, and I'll take it from there."

The young woman nodded, then handed Gem a key card. "Your room is down the hall. I've kept you on the main floor, but put you on the far side of the hotel away from the bar. The rooms should be quieter over there."

Gem smiled her thanks and turned to grab her bags. David already had them hoisted, waiting for her to lead the way.

The room was bright, clean and much smaller than anything she'd ever stayed in before while traveling with her father. Gem flicked on the light in the bathroom and wrinkled her nose at the missing features. Hmmm, no bidet or heated towel bars.

"How long should I give you?"

She jerked from her observations to spot David standing beside the dresser, next to her suitcase. Gem considered for a moment before responding. "Half an hour?"

He left without another word. She closed the door, wondering at the diversity of people she'd met since leaving home that morning. The whole experience was rather thrilling.

A hotel room, all to herself. Another first in her books. She was determined to make this trip overflow with new adventures.

Gem took one more slow revolution to examine her surroundings. A queen-sized bed, a couch against the wall. Small television, generic curtains and artwork. Surely there was more—there had to be. Her maid's room was larger than this.

There—across from the bathroom—another wooden door with a deadbolt. Gem twirled the lock and tugged the door inward, waiting with anxious anticipation to see...

Another door. This one with no doorknob. Gem pushed on the wood, but nothing budged. What kind of strange world was the Yukon that they had doors that led nowhere? She closed the door on her side of the room, suddenly aware she was wasting time. She pressed the latch shut and jumped as her cell phone rang.

"Poop." Daddy's ring tone. Her cheeks flashed hot at being caught swearing, kind of, as she dug in her purse for her phone. She simultaneously snapped on the answer button and reached for the zipper on her suitcase. She had less than twenty-five minutes before David returned.

"Gemmita? Everything okay, little girl? You were supposed to phone as soon as you arrived."

She bit back the retort she wanted to voice. My, she must be a lot more tired than she expected. Either that, or there was something in the northern air that had erased all her manners. "I was about to ring. I haven't been here long. As a matter of fact, I've just checked into my room."

"You can change your mind about this. You don't have to prove anything to me, sweetie."

*Arghhh*, fathers. Was she ever going to be more than a child to him?

"I'm fine, Daddy. And I want to do this. The trip is an exciting part of my education, and a real opportunity to put my training into action." His silence on the other end of the line did nothing to increase her happiness. Gem shucked her shoes and stockings, digging one-handed into her suitcase to find fresh underclothes while placating her parent. "I have some sightseeing planned, the northern flight is already booked. I've got all my equipment arranged—everything is in place. You knew a field excursion was a part of my schooling when I signed up."

"I expected you would conduct your research somewhere in Georgia, not in the middle of nowhere, hundreds of miles from home."

Gem tucked her phone into the crook of her neck and awkwardly held it in place. She'd even surprised herself with the radical idea. Finding a research topic that forced her to go to the Yukon?

She'd anticipated he'd be upset.

"I know you'll miss me, but everything will be fine. It's three weeks, four at the tops, and I'll have the information needed to finish my paper. Plus, this project should give me a good shot at getting that job with the company you approved of."

"You don't need to work." His change of tack was a resumption of the oldest argument they'd ever had, starting well before her mother had passed away.

Gem hopped on one foot as she pulled on new silk stockings. "I'm not having that discussion, Daddy, so stop. I'll be home within the month. If you want to contact me, use email. Otherwise, please, let me do this? I am capable, of this and more."

The alternative was to admit she was nothing but a piece of spoiled fluff like she'd overheard her fellow students declare. It wasn't true—there was so much they didn't know about her, things that she chose to go along with simply to keep the peace. But now? She had to see this project through to the end.

Her father sighed, long suffering in his tone. "Yes, Gemmita, I'll let you go. I want you to phone me the instant you need anything, you understand? Anything. What the hell good is having money if I can't use it to make sure you're comfortable and happy?"

She forced a laugh. "I love you. I'm going to enjoy every minute of the adventure, okay? And I'll tell you all about it when I get home."

She blew him a kiss then scrambled to tuck the phone away and finish getting dressed. Only, what should she wear? At home, meeting an Alpha was a formal event, with all the highest-level pack in attendance. Not to mention she had broken protocol—groveling could be a messy business if she didn't set the right tone from the start.

Gem eyed the clothes she'd purchased for her upcoming fieldwork and wrinkled her nose. Nope. Sturdy canvas and baggy cotton would not do. She dug deeper into the suitcase and went for the high-powered artillery, fingers crossed the Alpha was single and at least remotely interested in females.

Wrapping dazzled males around her little finger and making sure they weren't aware of it was one area in which she had some experience.

# Chapter Two

After half an hour in Evan's office, Shaun was feeling better than he had in weeks. Months even. The liquor in the dusty bottle had been poured into teeny tiny glasses, and he'd shot back the first round in one toss. Evan's brows hit the ceiling right about the time Shaun's brain lit on fire.

"Most people sip it, dude."

"Shit." His throat was melting, his tonsils had incinerated. They might be able to figure out how old he was if there was anything left of his teeth to carbon date.

But now that it seemed a good ninety-five percent of his blood was pumping with that same fiery fluid, Shaun didn't have a care in the world, or a discreet tongue in his head.

"I mean, life sucks. All my friends got mates, man. And I'm alone in the dark hangar with nothing but flipping my helicopter to keep me warm."

Evan frowned. He started to speak a couple of times, stopping as if confused.

"Wassup?" Shaun's tongue had grown thicker, and his words weren't flowing so good. The windows wiggled in the walls.

Cool. He'd never seen windows do that before.

"You're doing what to your helicopter?"

Shaun paused in confusion. It had to be the liquor. Evan had clearly lost his mind. "What?"

"You were flipping your helicopter."

Was his Alpha going deaf? Such a sad thing to happen to such a young man. Shaun spoke slower, and trifle louder—just in case that would help. "I hit and fuck chopper, and fly hangars in the dark."

Evan nodded. One of those *go along with the crazy person— let's not agitate him* nods. The fact Shaun had seen that kind of response so many times it was instantly recognizable kinda burned.

"I'm trying to imagine how the hell you're masturbating that you call it a helicopter. Sounds painful."

*What in the world?* Shaun rushed to explain, even as his tongue tangled further. "No, no, I'm flying my hangar. Wait, I mean, I'm shitting in my hanging, ducking my flapping heli." He slammed a hand over his mouth. *Damn.* His brain cells had melted into a lump of jelly. Or Jell-O. Wiggling neon Jell-O with raspberries floating in the middle layer...

He shook his head and attempted to focus both eyes on the same point. Nope—not happening. The room did one slow revolution counterclockwise, and he stared upward, expecting to spot a disco ball or something dangling from the ceiling to explain the sparkling lights flashing on the walls. Wolf metabolism usually dealt with alcohol in a quick and efficient manner. His didn't seem to be working tonight. Shaun snatched the bottle off the table, the blue glass swelling and shrinking before his eyes. "What. The hell. Is this shit?"

Evan sprawled in his La-Z-Boy and took another sip. Every muscle relaxed, contentment oozed out from him like a cat that had fallen into a bucket of cream after tormenting the dog. "Moonshine, from my old pack. Doubles as rocket fuel."

"*Fuckit.*" The room spun quicker. "Freak me out. I mean, get me drinked?"

"You may as well sit and be quiet for a bit." Evan peered at him, shaking his head in disgust. "Here I thought you could hold your liquor. Sad. Sad state of affairs."

Shaun would have argued, but right now there was this super interesting crack in the ceiling that grew, sprouting mosaic arms of purple and chartreuse. He leaned back in his chair to get a better view, reaching down to tug the recliner arm and raise the footrest, like he'd seen Evan do.

The next minute these really cool glowing lights were dancing in front of his eyes.

"Shaun, that's not a recliner."

Shaun reached to his side and tapped. Solid wood boards met his fingers. His back was well supported, legs stretched out. The room now spun in the opposite direction. "Did I fall down?"

"And you can't get up again."

"Cool. I'll just...you know, hang out for a bit. Okay with you?"

Evan laughed. "Sure. Only next time? Sip the 'shine, got it?"

"No prob."

It was kind of comfy on the floor. Evan rose and lit the fire, warmth pouring from the hearth to pool past where Shaun lay.

"Hey, did you..." Shaun lost track of the words. Why was he here again?

It wasn't because he was bored. No, he was sure there were plenty of things he was supposed to do. He had Maxwell's Silver Hammer, the aviation company he co-owned with a buddy. A full summer schedule approaching where he'd be busy providing helicopter trips over the most beautiful part of the world. Sightseeing and supply dumps, and the occasional medical emergency—he did them all. So why did he feel like crap?

Oh. Right. His friends were deserting him.

"You ever get lonely, Evan?" Shaun scrambled to his feet then held out his glass to his Alpha who carefully poured him another two fingers' worth. Shaun eyed his chair, the one on the floor, and decided the couch appeared a trifle more sturdy.

"I find it fascinating what topics I hear when I serve the good stuff. No, Shaun, I'm never lonely. I have all the pack around. And friends, like you. Although, I'm not sure why I'm trying to talk to you anymore. You're so pissed right now I could tell you anything I want and you'll never remember a word in the morning."

"Really?" His hand shook. The liquid in his glass sloshed and Shaun lapped the spilt alcohol off his fingers carefully. It wouldn't do to make a mess in his Alpha's office. "Then tell me big secrets, man. The kind of stuff you don't share with anyone, but think about when you're all alone..." *sniff* "...alone. Like me. Fuck."

There was a reason he wasn't supposed to do this, but he couldn't remember the specifics. He held the glass to his lips and tossed his head back. An icy sensation bled down his throat, seconds before the cold morphed into daggers stabbing his brain from the inside out.

"Shaun! Damn fool, that's it, you're cut off."

The glass disappeared from his fingers. The same fingers that glowed in a wonderful Aurora Borealis imitation. It was as if all the flames he'd consumed were attempting to escape from his body through his skin.

The visuals were either very cool or very creepy.

The cushions of the couch reached up fluffy fingers to cradle him tighter, and Shaun sighed. Evan's face appeared in his line of vision, the man's dark hair waving as he shook his head.

"I know it's strong, but, damn. You have the worst tolerance for moonshine of any shifter I've ever met." Evan hauled a chair over, the feet screeching on the wooden floor. The shiver up Shaun's spine exploded out his ears.

"Ouch."

Evan leaned back and crossed his arms. He cupped his chin for a moment then dropped his hand to point at Shaun.

"You know what your problem is? You don't have a mission."

"I need a mission?" *Cool.* Didn't know that was a requirement of the Takhini pack.

"Something to give you a reason to get up in the morning. Shaun, I've watched you since you settled back in Whitehorse. You're listless. You fight if you have to, but you don't enjoy it, not even when you win."

"I always win."

Evan nodded. "Of course you do, because you're a strong wolf. But you succeed without even trying. It's easy for you to win against the punks who come to try you. The more experienced wolves avoid you—they know you're strong, even if you are a little stupid."

"Hey—"

"Because you're not fighting to become a leader in the pack. You're simply fighting to fight." Evan shook his head and that finger popped out again. Shaun tried tracking the shaking object, but he found it damn near impossible to tell which was the real finger amongst the liquor haze.

Okay, this was interesting, but a bit too much like therapy.

"I don't want your job," Shaun blurted out. Hell would be preferable to run. At least demons were predictable, unlike wolves who were endlessly creative in coming up with new mischief to try.

"You don't want my job." Evan shot back, his confidence screaming out.

Shaun hesitated. "Did we already have this conversation? It sounds familiar."

"You don't want to be Alpha, Shaun. You'd have to actually give a damn about someone then."

Ouch. The words percolated through the alcohol haze, and a thin line of cold ran up his core. "What a fucker of a comment. If I'm that much of an asshole, why did you let me return to the pack?"

"Because at the root of it, you're only an asshole because you don't give a damn about yourself right now either, and I'm getting annoyed at your stupid refusal to grow up."

*Okay, that was one step too far.* "And did you get this special bullshit training in Alpha school or—?"

Suddenly Evan was right in Shaun's face, and he couldn't budge. Evan had him pinned in a neck hold, trapping his body against the couch. There was no air getting through his windpipe, and Shaun scrambled his fingers over Evan's forearm. Stars appeared in front of his eyes, glowing even brighter than the mysterious Northern Lights clouding everything else in the room.

"Don't mistake my tolerance for weakness." Evan hissed in his ear. Dangerous. Shaun fought back as hard as possible and barely moved. Evan held him immobile. "You're a damn good wolf, and I'm getting tired of seeing you waste your life. You don't need to want to save the world, but you need to care enough to do what's right for more than simply a lark."

Blessed air flooded into his lungs as Evan released him, settling him back into the couch's soft surface. Shaun stared at his Alpha, shocked nearly sober—well, maybe not that. Definitely chastised enough to remember a few manners, though.

"I'm...sorry."

Evan shrugged. "I am too. I don't usually lose my temper." He retook his seat, sipping his moonshine as he stared into the fire. "You need to face it, Shaun. We're wolves. We like having a pack around, but there are times it's not the pack we long for."

*Fuck.* Shaun didn't think he'd told anyone about the ache in his gut for a mate. For the feeling of truly belonging. "Have I been talking in my sleep or something?"

Evan shook his head, holding his glass up to the light after a quick sip. "Love it when this stuff kicks in and people lose track of whole threads of conversation. No, Shaun, you told me a few minutes ago. You're lonely. You'd give anything to find your mate. But in the meantime, you're going to be the best damn wolf there is, and get off your ass and do something for someone else who can't possibly repay you."

Shaun sniffed. "My God, I'm so charitable. Is that really what I said?"

Evan leaned forward on his elbows and nodded seriously. "I was very impressed, my friend. And you said you would start right away."

"Awesome." *Wow.* He had a purpose in life. A goal, and he was going to be a hero to...someone. His throat tightened with emotion—delight, determination...confusion. There was one trouble. The only things in his mind were the delightful pink and purple clouds morphing into elephants and crashing rhinos right before his eyes. "Did I tell you *what* I was going to do?"

"Not a word. Top secret, all that shit. But I'm sure you'll let me know when it's appropriate."

"Cool." Shaun relaxed back into the cushions. There was something so right about hanging out with Evan. "I love you, man."

Evan choked on his drink, his face turning bright red as he coughed his lungs out for a second. His expression transitioned to one worthy of a long-suffering and indulgent older brother. "That's great. Now I think you are ready to crash for the night."

Shaun peeked at his watch. The digital numbers were impossible to see, but he pressed onward. Faking it worked for many things. "Oh my, is that the time? I'm going to turn into a pumpkin."

Evan nodded slowly, his expression twisting into an evil grin. "Sure you are, big guy. Six thirty is oh-so-late for a weeknight. Tell you what. I'll pop you into one of the empty hotel rooms."

*Brilliant.* His Alpha was the most brilliant man he'd ever met. "Good idea." Shaun stood then dropped to a low crouch to counter all the heaving underfoot. "Fuck—is that an earthquake?"

Evan clicked his tongue like a mother hen, grabbed him by the arm and dragged him out the back exit and down a side hall. "Trust me, it's not the floor that's shaking."

He swiped a keycard and pushed open a door.

Mercy sakes, that was a king-plus bed, and the enormous thing was calling his name *soooo* sweetly. Shaun turned and impulsively hugged Evan. "I love you, man," he repeated.

"You probably aren't going to like me very much in the morning but, yeah, fine. I love you too. Now sleep it off, dude."

Blessed darkness beckoned, and Shaun strolled forward,

stripping as he went. Before the outer door clicked shut behind him, he yanked back the covers and collapsed face-first onto the mattress, a groan of pleasure escaping his lips.

This was better than his single bed back at the hangar. Far better than the bunk in the clan house in town. The only thing that would make his situation better yet? He sniffled and ignored the thoughts cavorting around in his mind singing in three-part-harmony about how nice it would be to have a soft feminine touch in his life.


She'd given up making her hair cooperate, and had finally managed to pull the dark strands back into a plain but presentable bun when a knock sounded. Gem smoothed her palms over the knee-length peach-coloured silk skirt, straightening to tug the neckline of her matching cashmere sweater a trifle lower. She squared her shoulders and adjusted her handbag before opening the door.

David flashed a brilliant grin as he checked her out.

"Now that's a nice outfit. Evan will be impressed." The cabbie-slash-philosopher-slash-guide offered his arm, and she slipped her fingers over his elbow without hesitation. "Let me lead you through the chaos—don't mind the boys, okay?"

The volume cranked way up as they passed the bar doors and the ambience changed from modern classic to turn-of-the-century madhouse. The room was full of bodies, mostly shifters if her nose had anything to say. Some of them danced on the tiny floor, some played darts, but most stood around tall tables or perched on high stools eating and laughing and hanging out.

From the table closest to her, one of the men rose to his feet, his gaze crawling over her as if she were naked. Gem stumbled for a second before David pulled her upright, slipping his body between her and the new threat.

Funny how the cabbie had gone from being a stranger to someone she felt would protect her.

"Knock it off, Jackson."

"Just wanted to make sure the lady got a proper northern welcome."

David tugged her toward the back of the pub. All around them excitement trembled in the air—the energy in the bar was wild and energetic, and in spite of the tinge of uncertainty inside, she'd never felt more alive.

Independence was heady stuff.

"Evan's back in his office. Come on, darling, you don't fit in with this crowd."

Gem stared in fascination at one of the women on the dance floor. The top buttons of her blouse hung open, the swells of her breasts visible to everyone. She twirled and her mini skirt rose, revealing a tiny thong and bare butt cheeks. Gem's face flushed hotter than a summer day. There went the idea that her own outfit was provocative. Obviously, she was mistaken.

No, she didn't belong here, that was clear.

David knocked on the door, again placing himself as a barricade between her and the action in the room.

A tenor rang out from the other side. "What?"

"Visitor from the States."

A longish pause. "Come in."

Gem slipped past David into the warm office, and peace settled. The fire in the hearth, the leather furniture—this room wasn't her home, but a lot more comfortable than the rowdiness occurring in the bar.

"Evan, this is Gemmita Jacobs, from Georgia. She's the one

Shaun's taking north in a few days for that Porcupine Herd analysis."

Gem startled. "Hey, how did you—"

"There are many ways to find out information when it's needed." David tipped his hat and pointed into the room. "Evan Stone. He's a good bloke. You'll be all right. I'm sure I'll see you later."

David left in a whirlwind, and Gem turned to take her first look at the Whitehorse Alpha.

Dark hair neatly trimmed around his ears, snapping black eyes that examined her with sharp intelligence. He was all lean muscle, bright white teeth, the entire appealing package sprawled in a low leather chair. One leg bounced, his knee hanging over the armrest, his foot rocking steadily to the low-lying beat of music sneaking in under the door. The position left his torso wide open, and she snapped her gaze back to his face before she continued staring anywhere inappropriate.

His smile twisted to one side, and he raised a brow.

Gem flushed. So much for keeping her arrival inconspicuous and politically correct. He'd caught her gaping at his groin. How gauche.

"Sorry for not getting up, but I've had a hell of a day." He gestured to the couch across from him. "Have a seat. I won't keep you long. You must be tired."

Gem dipped her head. She'd never met an Alpha quite like him before, but she could get around that. *Act normal, you idiot. Charm him—smooth out this mess.* "I apologize for not letting you know sooner I would be in your territory. I'm terribly embarrassed."

She sat, and a curious scent surrounded her. Something that made her catch her breath and a tingle start deep, deep inside. She tried to hide her reaction, but Evan narrowed his gaze.

"What? Why are you wrinkling your nose like that?"

Another flash of—excitement? need?—rushed over her, and she opened her mouth to explain away her rudeness with some kind of cast-off remark when a flicker of comprehension singed her.

The aroma made her mouth water, and her heart race. She reached up and tugged on the neckline of her sweater, finding the collar suddenly far too constricting. She wanted nothing better than to strip the fabric away and go down to bare skin. Let the air play over her and have fingers touch everywhere. Her breasts felt heavy, her sex pulsed with a steady rhythm, growing wet.

Only one thing made a wolf react like this—as if she'd been involved in hours of foreplay instead of having spent minutes in his presence.

"I don't mean to be rude, but there's this scent…" She took another deep breath, and it was as though the crisp air shot straight from her nose to her clit, her body going all soft and needy.

*Oh my goodness.* This couldn't be…could it?

She cleared her throat. Maybe she was overtired from the trip. But that shouldn't be enough to make her react as if she was in the midst of a sexual encounter.

Was Evan her mate?

The notion terrified her. Not because she didn't expect a life partner to appear some day, but finding her mate right now would cause a lot of trouble. One more issue to deal with while she fought for independence. And an Alpha whose territory was a fifteen-hour flight away from home? *Oh boy.* Daddy would have kittens.

But something was up, and ignoring the possibilities wouldn't change the answer.

Enough with the being-a-coward thing. She waved a hand between them. "I wonder if you'd mind...?"

The confusion on his face smoothed away as awareness filled his eyes. He leaned forward in his chair, elbows to knees as he breathed in deeply, nostrils flaring. He *hmmed* lightly, his tone a little lust-filled. Gem sucked in a quick breath in response, and the whammy smacked her between the legs again. She squeezed her knees together instinctively, and he grinned.

"Come here, darling. I don't think I'm what you're looking for, but I have no objection."

He patted his lap.

Gem stilled. He wasn't serious, was he? And yet, if he was her mate, she was seconds away from one of the most important moments of her entire life.

Grace. Elegance. That's what she'd bring to this occasion. Even as she rose to her feet, she straightened her spine and smiled properly. Stepped to his side and pivoted. Oh my, the wonderful aroma continued to fill her nostrils, and her body's involuntary response to its effect added another layer of scent to the room. Excitement filled her limbs, making them tremble in anticipation of his touch.

She sat slowly, hard thigh muscles meeting her backside. Her eagerness increased. Need raged inside for another zing of lust to shoot through her body. Like holding a wick of desire toward a flame in the hope unquenchable passion would envelop her.

Evan settled her against his torso as he leaned back, drawing her face closer. His lips hovered near. A slow approach, maddening.

His fingers in her hair, chest to her breasts. She closed her eyes as their mouths connected.

# Chapter Three

Gem was so dainty as she plopped into his lap. Evan had to admit this was the most interesting meet-and-greet he'd had in his relatively short time as Alpha for the Takhini pack.

The scent of her desire rose around them, making him feel slightly dirty. Oh, he liked having a long, lean honey panting over him. Especially one like this, with her soft brown skin, huge dark eyes that had grown even bigger when she'd caught a whiff of something in the air. Only, while she was delightful to look at, all smooth hourglass curves with endless legs and an elegant neck—she wasn't his type. Too delicate, too fine, and definitely not catching his notice in terms of being his mate.

Which is what he'd picked up from her stumbling question. Something made her think he might be the one, and while he had no interest in forever, he'd be happy to let her be the one to call it quits today. Shouldn't take too long—once he didn't make her motor run, she would no doubt stop their intimate contact.

Of course, if this was some southern custom of greeting the ruling Alpha with a tumble—hell, who was he to argue with tradition? It wasn't as if he didn't get all kinds of intriguing offers from the local wolf ladies, based solely on his position. Having a visitor to do the mattress mambo with would be far less complicated than his current dilemma of keeping the power-seekers in check.

She kissed him back. Innocent, chaste, lips closed and pressed to his.

Forget that. Even if they were mates, a simple kiss wouldn't be enough to confirm or deny their connection. While the scent on the air told him she was turned on, her reaction wasn't in response to his touch. He needed her to know for sure—as in *no way in hell are you my mate* for sure.

A little more thorough encounter was required.

He grasped the back of her neck as he angled her head to the side, teasing the seam of her lips with his tongue until she opened to him.

Hmm, much better. With a hesitant touch, all warm and soft, she explored his mouth, her hands rising to cup his face, and he smiled. The kiss grew more heated, teeth and lips getting involved as she twisted in his lap, her chest rubbing his.

*Oh, nice.* Maybe she wasn't too delicate after all. Evan withdrew his right hand from her back, sliding up her torso to cup one perfect breast, and she gasped against his lips. He soothed her, even as his thumb brushed the tightening tip of her nipple. She had nice firm mounds that he was sure would look spectacular if he stripped her. He gave a brief moment to consider what colour her nipples were, but his curiosity was nothing more than a typical male reaction to a desirable female. Nothing earth shaking or undeniable.

As far as he was concerned, this was fun, but not a forever mate-need-want-gotta-have situation.

Gem planted a hand on his chest and pushed, her lips separating from his with a soft sigh. There was a crease between her eyes and confusion on her face. He froze his hand and smiled back at her.

The little throat clearing that followed was kinda cute. "I…don't feel anything."

Hell, hiding his smirk was going to kill him. "Nothing?"

Her mouth opened to a shocked O. "It's not that I don't find you attractive, and I was enjoying—" Her gaze dropped to where he still grasped her breast. Embarrassment poured from her far stronger than lust, and Evan relented and withdrew his hand without a word.

But when she would have squirmed away he held her for another moment, releasing a trace of his wolf power to calm her. She lifted her gaze to meet his, and he touched her cheek. "You're a lovely wolf, but you're not mine. Don't worry, we'll figure out what's up. Please, though, allow me to offer the protection of my pack while you're in the north."

Her brown eyes were enormous as she stared back. Making her part of his responsibility wasn't necessary, but the offer felt right, especially after groping her. She might have walked into his office looking as if she owned the world, but she was a long way from home. Whatever physical mischief was happening— she needed a little reassurance and his Alpha genes had kicked into high gear.

Evan expected her to retreat as quickly as possible, but she surprised him by leaning in and kissing his cheek. "Thank you. For the offer of protection, and for allowing me to...satisfy my curiosity. I'm not sure what's wrong."

He helped her rise, supporting her until she regained her feet. "Anything unusual happen on your flight? You come in contact with any other wolves between arriving and now who caught your interest?"

"Nothing on the flight. I got a ride here with the cabbie, David, and I didn't react to him at all. Since then I've been in my room waiting—they told me you were busy."

*Oh hell.* And who had he been busy with? The only other wolf who'd been in his office today for long enough to leave a scent signature was Shaun.

Evan kept his face blank as the possibilities smacked him up the side of the head. This was getting more and more interesting. Was the princess panting over Shaun? "I think..."

She had taken a seat across from him on the couch, and watched with keen interest. Knees together, ankles delicately crossed, back straight. Add a china cup and a fancy hat, and she could have been at home having tea with the Queen. How was she going to take the news that her potential mate was three-sheets-to-the-wind at the moment?

How bad was Shaun going to flip? The guy had been almost crying like a girl over the fact he was all alone, but what kind of a woman had he been imagining as a mate? Evan eyed Gem again, and his sense of humour poked him hard. Maybe he *should* send her to Shaun's room. Instant contact was the simplest way to figure out if there was some mate-ish stuff in the cards for the mismatched couple.

His common sense battled back and hog-tied the hysterical images of Gem and Shaun meeting right now, and forced him to consider the good of the pack and his commitment as Alpha.

Damn, sometimes having to be a grown-up sucked.

Gem waited for him to finish speaking, curiosity and more in her expression.

Evan rose to his feet and held out his hand to her. "I think the answer will have to wait for a little while. Come. I'll buy you a late supper, then in the morning I'll take you to someone who should be able to answer your questions."

She hesitated before nodding. "If you think that would be best."

His timing wasn't what she wanted to hear—Evan sensed her frustration. But waiting was all he was willing to provide tonight, and she was far too polite to make a fuss. Lovely thing about well-bred young ladies, that. He led her to the bar, and let the anticipation of the fun and games coming tomorrow entertain his imagination.

Lordy, but she ached. The scent that had been driving her mad dissipated once they left Evan's office. The kick-start to her libido was more difficult to turn off. Tucked into the corner of the pub with the music pulsing in time with the beat raging between her thighs, she was hard-pressed to remain aloof.

"Wine?"

Gem dragged her attention back to Evan. Wine? *Oh, that was a question.* She nodded.

Evan spoke to one of his waitresses, turning back to raise a questioning brow. "Would you like bison? Or salmon?"

Her mind whirled too hard to concentrate. "Please—whatever you decide will be fine."

He patted her hand, nodding as if he understood her dilemma. Her gaze returned to the room around them as he finished ordering. Everywhere she looked there was something to catch her interest and increase her arousal. At the table opposite them a couple kissed, long and slow, infinitely erotic as their tongues brushed together. An electric tingle struck deep inside as she spotted two wolves leaning against the wall, one covering the other as he nuzzled his partner's neck. The dance floor was filled, body to body, all gyrating and pumping in a wild enthusiastic celebration of life.

It was terribly hot. Gem patted her napkin over her forehead and neckline. She drained her water glass, and still the heat rampaging through her system refused to cool.

She'd already decided this was one of the most unusual

evenings she'd ever spent when the constant stream of, for lack of a better term, hussies parading past their table began. No less than a dozen women came over. Supposedly to welcome her, but it was clear enough after the second faked casual *hello* they were there to see if Gem was a challenge to their hopes to hitch up with the Alpha.

Even in her mind-fuddled state, she was shocked. Some women would go to any lengths for attention, but this kind of approach was far too blatant to be effective. Getting your way around the male of the species, human or wolf, took a little more finesse.

Evan appeared uncomfortable with the whole situation. When he managed to scatter the final of the convoy like the squawking crows they were, he tossed Gem a less-than-in-control grin.

"Sorry about that. Ignore them."

"Do you get this much attention from women all the time?"

"Well..."

His bravado was back, his expression changing as she stared at him, and the kiss they'd shared returned in vivid detail. She flushed. "I mean, not that I don't think you're attractive. You are, very, but..."

The tension between them dissipated as they both laughed. Evan winked. "Why, thank you. But yeah, it's part of the hardship of having a high-ranked position and no partner."

Gem considered his dilemma. "What would they have done if we had turned out to be mates?"

He paused in the middle of lifting his glass to his mouth. "How good are you at arm-wrestling?"

She smiled. "Is that a northern euphemism for displays of power?"

Evan nodded.

*Interesting.* Back home they all knew their place. There was little movement up or down the ranks in the pack, and everything stayed very dignified and orderly. Getting asked to show how strong she was—that hadn't happened in a long time.

She rested her fingers on the back of his hand. "Excuse me if I break any rules—this isn't a common situation for me."

His sexy grin flashed. "Trust me, darling, there's not much you could do to surprise me."

She shrugged. Wolf hierarchy games had never thrilled her. She opened the mystical part of herself and let a smidgen sneak out. Just a tiny bit, like she had back at the airport.

Well, that was the intention. Maybe she was more tired now, or the confusion of the strange scent had affected her ability to maintain control. This time her power didn't sneak, it ripped through the pub like a low-level sonic boom. All faces whipped in their direction. A few wolves fell to their feet. Chairs tipped as bodies scrambled back, eyes wide with...fear?

*Oops.*

"I have no idea why—" Sheer embarrassment heated her face, again. It seemed she was going to spend her entire time in the Yukon either aroused or embarrassed. Or both.

Evan stared slack-jawed for a minute before breaking out into a deep, strong laugh that shook the room harder than her momentary loss of control. He rose to his feet, turning with his palms open, his confidence streaming out like a calming balm.

"Relax, it's okay. Everything is fine."

The pack members dipped their heads, then turned back to their activities, music resuming. The overall tone in the pub remained subdued for a few minutes, with an awful lot of questioning glances tossed their direction.

The receptionist from the front desk, Caroline, popped in the doorway and glared at Evan. She rolled her eyes before making her way to a table occupied by a human couple. Gem overheard her commenting to them about music systems and overload feedback.

Great. She'd made the Takhini pack have to do damage control around humans. She was toast. She was going to be sent home on the first plane south, without a chance to complete her research.

"I stand corrected. That was not what I expected." Evan's tone was light, but a tad more respectful than before. Maybe.

She struggled to apologize enough to make up for her blunder. "I'm so sorry. I had no intention of making a public display that loud."

He shrugged. "I've always been told it was the quiet ones to watch for, and in your case, that's true. You pack a pretty punch there, sweetheart. Not quite as powerful as me though..." Evan polished his fingernails against his shirt, before tossing her an outrageous wink.

Forgiven? That easily? "I'm not in trouble?"

He pushed her empty water glass away to make room for the arriving plates of food. "No. No trouble. And thank you—all the women who have been hounding us should give me a bit of a reprieve, at least until you're out of town. They aren't going to mess with you, darling. Just in case, you know."

The rest of dinner passed in a blur. She didn't taste a thing, couldn't remember a word she said. When Gem finally closed the door on Evan's grin she was more confused than the last time she'd been alone in her hotel room.

Only her years of training in etiquette had allowed her to sit and chat with the pulse of sexual desire firing through her veins. She turned and headed toward her suitcase, kicking off her shoes, stripping the confining sweater and skirt away. There were more than a few times she must have lost her concentration, if the amusement on Evan's face was any indication.

She was getting very tired of people finding her entertaining.

The aching need swirling around her refused to diminish. It was as if a shimmering layer of an aphrodisiac lay over her skin, from her toes to the top of her head. Nothing had ever turned her on like she was now.

And, Lordy, the music. The pounding beat drove lust hard. She still heard it, and in a flash, there was nothing she wanted more than to have passion surround her. Push her farther down the road toward an urgent release. She clicked on the radio and fiddled with the knobs until she found a local station with a similar rhythm.

There was a mirror mounted over the dresser, and she caught a glimpse of herself. Her light pink bra and panty set shone like pale cotton candy against her dark skin. She pulsed her hips in time with the music, letting her hands drift above her head in imitation of one of the women on the dance floor.

Only that lucky lady had a man opposite her, someone to stare in admiration. A partner to caress her, draw their torsos close and grind their bodies together to let the heat between them escape. Gem had nothing but this frustrating sexual urge and no one to ride it with.

Like usual.

She cranked up the volume then slipped back into position before the mirror to resume her dance. Fine. If she was alone, that meant she could go for it. Swing her body to the beat and do whatever she wanted. And if Evan found her a solution in the morning for her troubles, that was wonderful, but in the meantime...

If she had to take matters into her own hands, she had a lot of experience with that as well.


The faint scent of laundry soap rose off the bedsheets, and Shaun nestled deeper in the covers to make himself a nest. Hmm, that almost, but not quite, feminine fragrance. Some of his happy thoughts faded.

Female? There was no female in his room. Sadness slammed into him like an earth slide.

He sniffed harder. Man, whatever they washed the linens in not only smelled good, it kinda...turned him on. A momentary confusion scrambled his brain—and the idea he might have had a wee bit too much to drink passed by, waving madly. He ignored the mental suggestion, stuck his tongue out at it, in fact.

He was a wolf, damn it. He could hold his liquor.

One mad grope gathered the covers into his arms, and he buried his face in them to breathe deeply. The interesting scent vanished, covered by the cloying after-burn of dusty dryer sheets.

Nope. Nada. He sat up, the crumpled bed linens forgotten as he found his feet. The fragrance wasn't coming off the bed, the delicious aroma instead rolled along the covers, originating from somewhere else.

Shaun hauled himself off the mattress, the clock staring at him with red eyes complaining it was barely nine o'clock. He swung his head to peek out the window—pale light and not daylight bright. Okay, that meant evening, not morning, so he hadn't snoozed the entire night away yet.

There had to be a source to that wonderful smell. He was tempted to shift to a wolf—his sniffer would be stronger in that form, but doors were a bugger to manipulate with paws. Instead he clung to the wall to help stop the slow roll of...well, himself...as he made his way back to the main door.

Evan was a twisted bastard. Shaun grinned. The moonshine began to fade from his system as his wolf metabolism kicked into gear, but the wicked aftertaste remained, and the pounding in his head let him know he was going to hurt like the blazes.

Yeah, his Alpha was a right asshole—which pleased Shaun like whoa. The dude was the first Alpha he'd been beholden to whom he really respected when it came down to it. Just because a wolf was powerful enough to be able to boss around the rest of a pack didn't mean they had to lose their sense of humour like most of the tight-assed jerks who ran other territories.

Both hands slid onto a smooth surface, and Shaun halted. The connecting door to the next room was warm under his palms, a soft *thump, thump, thump* radiating from the opposite side. It took a little maneuvering to get the deadbolt undone, and he swung his door inward.

The second door, the one from the neighbouring room, remained closed, but the volume of the music and the amazing scent increased tenfold. Shaun soaked in the bouquet. Delicious and invigorating. Appetizing enough to chase away the brain-buster of a headache hovering nearby. One deep breath after another cleansed the fog from his brain and lit a direct path from his nostrils southward.

Whatever the hell was on the other side, he had to have a taste.

The music changed, slowing in pace. Shaun pressed his ear

against the door and froze in surprise as the surface retreated from him. He glanced to the side and spotted a faint crack of light glowing back. Holy shit—the lock on the second door was open, and as the space widened, he was gob-smacked with more of the mouth-watering goodness.

Leaning on the doorframe, he pushed and let the door swing on silent hinges away from him. His eyes adjusted to the increasing light, focusing in a flash as a pair of shapely cocoa-brown hips barely covered by pale pink panties swished from side to side not ten feet from him.

# Chapter Four

Shaun dug his fingers into the doorframe, using arm strength to keep his body vertical. Standing was a major issue in light of the reverberating shock waves rushing up his limbs. Every breath he took forced more of the incredible scent into his head and brain. His gaze remained trapped by the woman as she undulated before him, her head tilted to one side, her hands running over her skin. The long, lean line of her neck tempted him, the shimmer of the lamps highlighting her curves.

One pulsing beat after another, the music drove into his ears, his blood racing head to toe in powerful surges. And when she widened her stance and scooped upward with her palms, catching hold of her lace-covered breasts, Shaun wasn't sure what could possibly calm the storm raging inside him.

Imagining that he was touching her would be a good start, *him* pinching her nipples between his thumbs and forefingers. She hummed in time with the music just before the sound disappeared behind a scene of white noise, his hearing obliterated by the blood pounding out of his brain en route south to his groin. The lacy wisp of her bra floated to the floor, and he followed the frilly thing with his gaze, distracted for a second by the desire to pick it up and see if the lingerie was warm from her skin.

There had to be a reason for his entire body to be shaking with need. He glanced behind him into his room, his abandoned clothes untidy heaps barely visible in the darkness.

Was he still asleep? Shaun wiggled himself upright and pinched his thigh, snapping his mouth shut on the *ouch* he wanted to exclaim.

Nope. Awake.

A hallucination. That's what this was. Damn fine one too, made even more incredible the moment she revealed those breasts. Perfectly formed, dark nipples already tightened to peaks. Shaun stared slack-jawed, frozen in admiration for the sheer angelic beauty before him. Or maybe this was heaven— that was the answer. Evan's moonshine had given him a heart attack, and he was now entering the Pearly Gates. The cheap wooden doors weren't expected—but then people everywhere were dealing with cutbacks, right? And who the heck cared what the gates were made of when the streets beyond were lined with visions like this one.

He stepped forward and took a deep breath. Angelic perfume flooded his brain and erased all thoughts except needing to see if his other senses were going to be treated to an incredible feast tonight.

Then the angel opened her eyes, and he stared into dark glistening obsidian pools. Right before she vanished.

Gem snapped her mouth shut, trapping the scream that threatened to burst free. It wasn't turning to discover a man in her room—a *naked* man—that stunned her the most. The complete flip-flop her belly turned as her wolf sat up and howled in delight wasn't enough to shock her into letting a girlish cry escape.

It was staring into the man's eyes as all his humanity

drained away. Watching as he transformed into the biggest, most enormous and bushiest black wolf she'd ever seen in her life, the beast immediately crashing to the floor between the wall and the bed.

She snatched up her shirt and held the fabric in front of her. Then the stupidity of attempting to cover herself when she had a much bigger issue at hand hit—there was a strange wolf at her feet and her own itching to come out and say hello. Being mostly naked was nothing compared to that.

Gem took one step, then another, slow and cautious until she reached the end of the bed. She nudged one furry paw with her toe. "Hello? Are you okay?"

No response.

She peeked into the space behind the now open door, figuring out the rooms were pretty much identical. He'd opened his side, and she must have left hers unlocked. With that mystery solved, she turned back to deal with the more difficult one of the furry beast sprawled on her floor.

Deep inside she felt it again—a nearly violent urge to change and let her wolf crawl all over his. The scent in the air had returned to intoxicating levels, even higher than she'd experienced earlier in the office with Evan.

Oh my. *Oh no.* Through the haze of lust coating her mind like a thick coastal fog, the only possible solution pulsed out a lighthouse-warning signal.

Her mate? For real this time?

A low rumble bounced off the wall, urgent growls and moans increasing as the wolf scrambled to his feet. Gem retreated instinctively before making a stand.

She was not going to freak out. One hand shot forward, palm upright.

"Freeze right there, mister."

The wolf ignored her, pacing closer until he stood on top of her feet. Then he rubbed against her legs, bumping hard enough to force her to sit on the bed. The mattress swayed under her hips as he jumped up and joined her, the bulk of his wolf body dipping the surface.

He sniffed her cheek and sighed happily, the warmth of his breath hitting her squarely on the neck. Gem twisted to bring up one leg and face him better.

"You don't take direction very well, do you?"

A wolfish grin, with a full flash of teeth greeted her just before he stuck out his tongue and licked her from jaw to hairline.

She giggled and grabbed him. All thoughts of how utterly enormous his wolf was compared to the other wolves she knew disappeared as she wrestled with him on the mattress. Instantly comfortable with this stranger in her room, she targeted all the prime wolf ticklish spots, laughing as he squirmed under her.

Then he rolled and shifted at the same time, and instead of the weight of a furry wolf pinning her to the bed, the full length of a very smooth-skinned, muscular and naked man held her captive. His black hair hung in unruly tangles around his head, beautiful dark brown eyes with simply enormous pupils filling their cores hovered inches over hers.

A squarish jaw. The smile she'd seen moments earlier on his wolf—the expression was still there, although his teeth were now human-shaped and even. His nose had a slight bump in the middle, broken at some point she suspected.

"Hello, love."

His voice tickled inside her ears, drowning out the background music and sending an icy sensation down the length of her spine. She instinctively arched and hit the brick wall of his body. He held her immobile. His hips nestled tight to her groin, her breasts crushed to his chest.

The interest on his face flashed hotter.

Gem panted with need. She'd been turned on before, but now the scent in the air was an impossible-to-ignore aphrodisiac. "Hello. Are you...? I mean...are we...?"

He lowered his head and kissed the hollow of her neck. The icicles spread from her spine, threading in an intricate pattern over her skin. How could she be on fire and so cold at the same time?

"Are we what? Are we going to fuck?"

The dirty word was accompanied by a light nip to her throat, and Gem cried out. She thrust her hips forward, the rising heat between her legs meeting his erection. His very large erection.

Oh my goodness, they made everything about these northern wolves larger than in the south.

She tangled her fingers in his hair, reluctantly pulling his lips from where he'd been laying a trail of soft bites and lazy kisses.

"Stop. We need to stop for a moment. I don't even know your name."

He licked her bottom lip and moaned in approval. "Shaun Stevens. What's yours, princess?"

Shaun. Nice name. Gem found herself having difficulty speaking as he'd resumed kissing her jaw and the tender spot right under her ear. "Gemmita Ellen...Louise May...oh my, that feels wonderful...Jacobs."

He paused. Snorted lightly. "That's a bit of a mouthful, love. You have a shorter handle?"

"Gem. My friends call me—*oh!*"

A sharp pain struck, smearing into a wave of pleasure. The dangling earlobe where he'd nipped her throbbed in time with the ache between her legs.

"Pretty. Gem. Almost as pretty as you."

She smiled. Sweet-talking on top of the incredible rush of hormones dancing in her cells? This was going to be one extraordinary evening. A couple wiggles later, she was able to prop herself up on her elbows and stare at him. "Shaun?"

He twirled a fingertip around her right nipple as he rested on his other elbow, gaze fixed on hers. "Ah-huh?"

"Are we going to talk some more?"

Shaun leaned closer, his hand cupping the side of her breast, supporting her nipple skyward. He licked the tip. Once. Again.

"Later."

He closed his mouth around her and sucked. Electric impulses sparkled through her system, nerves going off standby and into highly sensitized and ready-to-explode mode.

Maybe talking was overrated. She relaxed back onto the pillow, her wolf rumbling its content as she smoothed a hand over Shaun's broad shoulders. His muscles shifted under her fingers as he played with her breasts, driving her with deliberate slowness to the brink of undeniable need.

All her earlier confusion faded. Making love with Shaun was right. Being with him was not only right, their meeting was the first thing in her life that had the potential to be perfect. Her mate, coming to claim her. She would claim him. Together, they'd be able to do anything.

All the stories of how much happiness there was found in having a partner were going to be true for her, starting this moment. Predestined mates might not be the human way, but her wolf inside basked in the attention, the total correctness of the situation.

Shaun licked her ribs. "I've dreamed about you."

She shivered.

"I never imagined you'd show up today. And now I can't stop touching you. Wanting you. Needing to bury myself in you." He dropped his forehead to her belly and she squirmed.

"Keep going," she begged.

Shaun looked her in the eye. "You'd have to kill me to make me stop."

That made them even. She'd kill him if he stopped.

His wolf wasn't far away—the beast was still visible in Shaun's eyes, in the way he went rigid at moments, as if fighting for control. Gem let a touch of her power escape to soothe him.

For one second the mystical connection worked. He relaxed, eased back into her arms. Then it was as if a totally impenetrable wall rose between them. Shaun's wolf vanished in that moment, and all that was left was the man who stared at her with extreme hunger in his eyes.

"It's not the wolves' turn, love. We'll let them out to play later. Right now, it's just you and me."

He lowered himself between her legs and touched her intimately with his lips. A soft caress to the inside of her leg. Another at the top of her curls.

When he slipped a finger along her slit, she realized something important.

"Shaun, you haven't kissed me yet. My lips, I mean—*oh...*"

One thick finger slid into her core as she spoke, and her question ended on a breathless sigh.

"Soon. Trust me." Shaun stroked in deep, the heel of his

palm rubbing the apex of her sex, his finger stretching her. "You're very tight. I don't want to hurt you."

"You won't." Gem spoke with utter conviction. He was her mate. There was nothing a mate wanted more than to make their partner happy. Even as she wondered how they would be able to juggle their lives, and locations, her momentary concerns faded.

He was touching her. How could she concentrate on anything but enjoying this moment?

The steady thrust of his hand into her core notched the tingling up to overdrive as he made additional contact—his mouth. He tongued the aching nub at the apex of her mound, lapping and licking in unending sweeps until she couldn't take it anymore. An orgasm ripped through her, shaking her, squeezing around the two fingers he'd carefully worked into her.

Gem pulled her knees farther to the side in expectation of him rising over her. He didn't shift position, but he kept moving all right—that talented tongue of his. She gasped for air as he stroked gentler now, forcing her to accept his touch until stars floated before her eyes. Moisture pooled around his fingers, her body loosening and wanting more.

"That's it, love. You're beautiful. Really and truly. The way you taste—hmm."

Shaun lapped again, sucking on her clit, and a long, slow pulse broke through. Gem quivered on the bed, wondering if she'd be able to walk when they were done. He hadn't stopped, but he hadn't given her what she needed yet.

She reached down and grabbed his hair, tugging harder as urgent desire rose. "Please. Take me, now. I need you inside."

His laughter rang out, a low rumble of amusement. "I need you too. But my wolf said to go slow."

*Really stupid, bad idea.* She tightened her grip and hauled him up to her level. She might be smaller than him, but she was still a wolf, and that made her strong enough to force even his bulk to change position.

"You said to leave our wolves out of this. If I want slow, I'll tell you."

There was a pause—only a second—as they stared into each other's eyes. Then the world exploded as they both moved.

He hadn't kissed her before. Now he consumed her, feasting at her mouth as if he was starving. She returned as good as he gave, nipping and licking, her tongue tangling with his. The exhilarating flavour of her mate burst onto her taste buds, adding to the richness of her pleasure.

They rolled together, the heat of his body pressed against her, the rigid length of his shaft nudging her thigh. Gem snuck down a hand and wrapped her fingers around him. Wide and solid and warm in all the right ways. She stroked in time with the thrusts of their tongues together, and he groaned into her mouth.

"Gem. Oh yeah, like that. Harder. Fuck—"

A shiver at the naughty word made her tighten her grip, and he threw back his head with a loud shout. She froze, fearful she'd hurt him, until reassured by his continuing enthusiastic thrusts forward.

Shaun broke free, brought her on top, clasping her so hard her muscles protested. She couldn't complain, not when he rearranged her and began a rocking motion, grinding against her ready sex.

"Now, please, please, please..." Gem tilted her hips, attempting to line them up properly. He refused to let go, maintaining the steady torment, driving her back up to the pinnacle. Each brush of his erection priming her body.

She pressed on his chest as she lifted her torso to vertical, catching his gaze. Her movement caused the tip of his shaft to slip through her folds. They hung together motionless—the place between worlds. Now they were two individuals—one step away from joining their lives forever.

The only sound was the song on the radio. Soulful, yearning.

He smiled up at her as he stroked her jaw with the back of his finger. "My mate."

*My. Mine.* The word thrilled her and scared her silly. Predestiny was the norm amongst wolves, but no one had told her how heart-stoppingly fragile facing this moment would make her feel.

One heartbeat passed.

Another.

Gem moved forward, Shaun thrust up, and the two of them connected forcibly. Mating heat danced around them like an exotic pied piper.

Instantly, she froze. The width of his erection stretched her, changed the ache of need into something midway between pleasure and pain. Similar to the nips and the bites he'd given, and she wasn't sure if she could survive if tonight got any better.

"Oh, Shaun." She leaned forward to kiss him. He lifted his head eagerly to allow his mouth to meet hers. The controlling grip on her hips loosened as he stroked her gently, fingertips soothing her. He tasted wild. There was raw energy in his kiss, the hint of a sweet aftertaste that made her smile against his lips.

The measured exploration of his hands continued as he slipped them farther up her torso to cup her breasts. Pulling in a breath of air from his mouth seemed the only way to get any oxygen. His palms were hot against her skin, the tender touch helping her relax. Slow smooth circles, teasing flicks over her nipples. The distraction on her breasts let her almost forget there was an extremely large section of his body currently in residence inside her.

Almost, but not possible.

Any pain she'd experienced was gone, replaced with the urgent desire to use him like a pogo stick. Gem tightened her thighs, lifted herself and moaned at how incredible it felt, the consuming rub that started deep and rose to the sensitive edge of her sex in line with the crown of his shaft.

"Sweet Gem. That's so good." Shaun's head thumped back on the pillow, his one arm thrown over his eyes, the other hand caressing her body. "I'm dying. I'm really and truly dying."

She rode him another time, the smooth stroke sparking energies inside her that wanted to break free. "You'd better not die. Other than your name, Shaun Stevens, I don't know anything about you."

His arm fell away, and the brilliant white of his smile hit her full force as she drove herself down harder. "I'm a wolf, you're a wolf. We're mates. That's all we need to know."

Mates. Another plunge. *Mates*. Together. This was really happening.

*"She's the most beautiful woman I've ever seen."*

Gem froze—sex forgotten. Well, kind of forgotten. It was difficult to completely ignore the fully erect penis in her passage, and that all manner of incredible hormonal things were happening because of that fact. And when Shaun took over and lifted his hips, increasing the pace between them again, Gem was the one to moan her approval in spite of having something to say.

"I heard you...in my head... Oh, Shaun..."

He didn't acknowledge her, the sheer bliss on his face enough to make her put the discussion aside and come back to what she was doing.

What they were doing.

Shaun smoothed his hands up her thighs, dipping his fingers between her legs to find the sensitive tip of her clitoris. He rubbed, and that was game over. Like pressing an ignition switch, the explosion was immediate and full body. Waves crashed upward, skimming her skin like a flash fire. Gem cried out and savoured the sensation.

Then he rolled her again, rising over her and taking total control. Thrusting into her, forcefully, madly. Each piston of his hips pressed her back to the bed. Gem wrapped her legs around him and canted her pelvis, a little scream escaping as he went deeper on the next motion. The climax that had started earlier went on and on, peaking higher and higher on each breath like consecutive firework bursts, each one more spectacular than the one before.

"Holy hell, Gem." Shaun slammed in once more and stilled. She felt every jerk intimately. Each hard pulse within her as her sheath squeezed him tight, wringing another cry from his lips.

Shaun lowered himself to lie skin to skin on top of her. The slow weight increase made her smile, a tender moment of complete satisfaction and delight all tangled up in the sated sexual bliss cocooning her body.

She had a mate. Incredible. Not just the sex, although that had been fairly spectacular to start with, but the realization she now had someone else in her life to love and care for. Gem traced her fingers over his back, the heat of having him close so right and proper.

A soft kiss landed on her lips, then he nuzzled her cheek. He dropped his full weight beside her and rolled them just enough that when he snored a moment later, Gem giggled then curled up tight to his side, joining him in sleep.

# Chapter Five

Caroline parked in her usual slot, right next to Evan's shiny red Hummer. She wasn't scheduled to work today, but this would be one of her only chances to catch the Alpha alone. The morning sunshine seemed to taunt her as she pulled her courage in and forced herself out the door toward the entrance to his suite.

Even knowing Evan Stone wasn't likely to hurt her, butterflies of fear still insisted on tangoing in her belly. What she was about to propose was extremely unusual—she knew that—but desperate measures were occasionally needed.

She squared her shoulders and knocked.

His footsteps sounded on the hardwood floor, and she pictured his approach with ease. She was the one who'd arranged for the renovations to the suite after he took over from their old Alpha. He was turning the corner, just about there...

"Caroline?" Evan opened the door and she caught an eyeful of rather spectacular masculinity. The jeans covering his lower body were nice, but it was the wolf genes he wore up top that made her libido jolt—his naked chest was oh-so-distracting.

It took a lot of self-control to concentrate enough to offer a smile. "Hey."

He looked her up and down slowly. Glanced over her shoulder. "Something wrong at the hotel I need to know about?"

She shook her head. "No, nothing. Everything's fine. I mean, things were fine when I left last night, and I didn't stop in yet this morning. I'm not on shift until tomorrow, to be honest, but I'm sure everything is going great."

Evan waited. Caroline bit her lip. She'd been rambling. That wasn't good. Wolves didn't like rambling. Straightforward, no nonsense. That had been her plan, but she always turned into a babbling fool when she got nervous.

*Nervous.* Shit—he could probably smell her anxiety. Damn wolf senses.

He stepped back, gesturing her forward. "You want to come in."

She was past him before she realized what he'd said. Caroline twirled to spot him sporting an ear-to-ear grin. "You already know why I'm here."

Evan closed the door behind them and laughed. "Caro, trust me. Of all the surprises thrown my way since becoming Alpha for the Takhini pack, *you* are the most interesting."

She followed him into the kitchen where she took a deep appreciative breath of the scent of coffee filling the room. Without thinking, she grabbed the coffeepot and two mugs, and prepped them both drinks. "What makes you say that?"

Evan tilted his head toward her. "Honey, you're the only human I know who would knock on my door at six a.m., walk in and make herself at home."

She paused. "Oh. Sorry."

He gestured for her to carry on. "I don't mind. Come on, let me know what's got you in such a tizzy this early."

She finished her task, passing him his mug. He'd found a T-shirt while she'd been working, and had covered up.

Damn it anyway.

The main living space was decorated with dark cushions scattered on thick log furniture. She'd had a blast putting the place together for him. The extra-wide windows faced the Yukon River, the curve to the left leading to the dry-docked *SS Klondike*. Only a few remaining pieces of ice clung to the edges of the river, and spring was well on its way.

Caroline turned from the view and grabbed a seat in one of the single chairs. Straight out with it—after all those years around her stepfather, you'd think she had this talking-to-wolves business down pat. "I have a proposition."

He sprawled on the couch, a contented smile breaking across his face as he took a large gulp of his coffee. "God, that is so good. How do you consistently make a perfect cup? Half the time my coffee tastes like dirt."

"You pour to the dregs and get all the excess grounds. You need to stop and leave a little in the pot." She watched his throat as he swallowed. "I want to move in with you."

Evan jolted upright, choking on his mouthful. She sat patiently, waiting until he calmed down. Except, every time he looked her direction, the coughing began again until she got pissed off. Placing her mug on the table, she stood, fists landing on her hips. "Fine. You don't have to spell it out. That's a no."

Before she'd reached the door he was there, blocking her path, his breathing still shaky. "You want to back this train up a few stations? I'm not saying no. I'm not saying yes. I'm saying what the hell kind of question is that?"

Caroline stared at the wall. "Was that too blunt? Johnny always told me to simply spit it out, that wolves liked the straightforward approach."

"Johnny. That's your stepdad, right?"

She nodded.

Evan wrapped an arm around her shoulder and led her

back to the living room, sitting next to her. This time he handed over her cup, motioning for her to drink. "Go on. Take a sip. We're not going anywhere until we get this figured out."

Caffeine was an utter necessity at this point, to get through the rest of the conversation. Evan reached past her and nabbed his own mug, his thigh pressing tight to hers. There was no way to hide her instant physical response, but she knew from their history he would simply ignore the way she heated up whenever he was near.

He was used to it, and frankly, she planned on making the undeniable attraction work in both their favours. She wasn't in love with him. Had no ideas of forever and all that kind of thing where Evan was concerned. The fact her secret agenda would be served nicely by getting a taste or five of his wolfish charms was a bonus in the scheme.

Guilt-free offers that helped both sides were always the best way to go.

They sat quietly and drank for a moment before Caroline deemed herself ready to try again. She placed her cup down and laughed when he copied her.

"Sorry, protective measures." Evan turned to face her. "Now. Seriously. Are you getting kicked out of your apartment and need a place to crash for a while?"

"No. I need to move in to stop the local women from tearing the town apart trying to get your attention."

His brow rose in the air. "You want to shack up for my sake?"

She nodded.

"But...you're not a wolf."

"I know. So you don't have to worry that I'm trying to do what all those other females are doing. Trying to get ahead in the wolf priority list."

Evan looked confused. "But you're not a wolf."

"Don't be stupid. I know that. Trust me, I got reminded of that often over the years by the rest of the pack every time they came around the house. Johnny was strong enough to fend them off until I learned to deal with them myself."

He leaned back and crossed his arms, Mr. Sexy in full view. "Well, sweetie, Johnny may have been right about shooting straight with wolves, but there are a few special circumstances when it's perfectly fine to explain yourself. In complete and utter detail."

"When would that be?"

Evan tweaked her nose. "When I can't understand what the hell you're proposing. I mean, I got the 'you move in with me' bit, but how will it help me having a human in my house?"

Caroline sighed. "The power plays are a constant thing, Evan. Add in the fact you're single, a looker, and a touch on the wild side, the ladies of the pack without boyfriends, and some with, are always trying to hit on you."

"I noticed. Why is that a problem for anyone but me?"

She pulled a face. "Okay. Take last night. I'm going to assume whatever happened in the bar was somehow related to the *woowoo* thing you guys do."

His grin got wider. "*Woowoo*. Nicely put. Is that the scientific word, or something we're still trying on for size?"

She ignored him. It was the only way to make this conversation go anywhere before she needed to drag in reinforcements.

"In the old days I had to come up with logical explanations for weird wolf shit happening around the hotel and bar maybe once or twice a month. And nine times out of ten the incidents were caused by visitors to the area—the usual gangly teens not able to control a shift, or thinking it would be hysterical to go for a swim in the pool in their wolf forms." Evan snickered, and she smacked him on the arm. "Laugh it up, big boy, but after a while trying to cover your asses and keep the shifters undercover is a royal pain. I like my job, and I like the pack. I don't like being your nursemaid."

"Sorry." He looked contrite enough, but his smile didn't diminish. "I was remembering the story they told me about you announcing there was a meeting for the Iditarod and some of the teams had gotten loose. That's why crowds of 'dogs' were swarming the halls."

Caroline sniffed. "That was one of my better moments of inspiration."

She stood and carried their empty cups to the kitchen, rinsing them and putting them in the dishwasher. When she stood, Evan was right there at her side.

"You didn't finish your explanation."

She leaned back on the island. "Think about it. Since you took over as Alpha, there have been more and more incidents. It's not once in a while anymore, it's weekly, if not daily. And the troubles are always related to a female panting over you in some shape or form. I realize jostling for position is normal for wolves, but it's a pain in the ass. As a human, I have no designs on your pack or being something big shot in the hierarchy. But with my background, I know enough about wolves to hold my own and keep the bitches off your back. At least until you tell me you've found someone you're interested in—I won't get pissed off if you announce it's over. I understand the whole mate thing."

Evan nodded slowly. "Makes sense. I'll think about your offer."

Caroline couldn't stop the little thrill of excitement that hit. "I can wait. Just try to decide before I have to explain a wolf fight in the front lobby, okay?"

He stretched and yawned. "Well, since we're both awake, you want to help me take a load to the recycle station?"

Hmm. *No.* "On my day off?"

"Who knows, there might be crowds of women waiting to leap out of the blue boxes and besmirch my virtue."

They both laughed, comfortable together in spite of her out-of-the-blue suggestion, and she could only cross her fingers and hope for the best.

There was a small headache crouched behind him, waiting to pounce. Shaun opened his eyes slowly, fearful of what he was about to discover. The last time he'd been this groggy when he woke, there had been hijacking, Russian fishing vessels and anvils involved. The ceiling looked unthreatening, but he didn't do anything stupid like move too fast. He never knew when a billowing black cloud would leap out and burst into a neon lightshow that would force him to squint in pain.

He hated these kinds of mornings, but had to admit they were fairly entertaining.

A soft purr of contentment sounded on his right, and he jerked. Then he cursed silently as the jerk triggered explosions that ricocheted through his brainpan.

He took his time and went for a slow roll. He only made it part way over. His legs were trapped, his hips tight against something warm and soft. Shaun leaned on one elbow to stare down at a one-hundred-percent, honest-to-God beauty-pageant winner.

She had the most incredible eyelashes. He wasn't used to spotting facial features first on a woman. Usually, it was her breasts or her legs he keyed in on. Being an equal-opportunity admirer of the female body, he hated to have a favourite part.

But this woman? Her lashes were like little furry caterpillars. Only—attractive caterpillars. He was tempted to touch one to see if it would crawl away, but he didn't want to wake her. She must be awfully tired after last night.

Whatever it was they'd done.

He had to assume that since they were in bed, naked—he checked—*yup*, naked—there had been some major mattress shaking going on. He really wished he could remember, because the sex must have been spectacular.

Shaun lay back and took a few deep breaths. Strangely, that didn't have the result he was looking for. His goal had been to relax and close his eyes until Miss Universe woke up and they could have a second, or third, round of whatever they had enjoyed before.

Nope, relaxing was out the window as soon as his brain registered what his nose said. It wasn't just how incredible her scent was, but the fact she smelled like him. He matched her, they were all mixed up and—*holy crap.*

"Oh my God, you're my mate." Shaun was up on his elbow again in an instant, staring at her. He racked his brains. Yesterday—fighting with bears, drinking with Evan, crashing at the hotel—he got that far. When the hell did *find your mate and fuck her silly* slip into the equation?

He wasn't sure if he should scream in joy or horror. He was so screwed.

She wiggled, brushing his side, and a shiver started where she made contact, the sensation racing all around his groin.

*Think. Think.* Shaun had to remember before she woke up,

because he was sure there was something in the female-wolf manual about permission to castrate your partner for forgetting your first time together. He'd forgotten a girlfriend's birthday once. It was kind of guaranteed that this would be an even bigger screw-up.

Maybe if he had a scorching hot shower. Or another couple stiff drinks. Shaun scrunched himself as small as possible before peeling backwards off the mattress with the same care he would use in disassembling a bomb. If he knew how to do such a thing.

One foot contacted the floor. The other. He used his hands to force his body upright, pleased to find he had no trouble staying vertical. She hadn't moved, the long strands of her hair wreathed around her head like a fluffy black cloud.

He liked how she looked, all soft and warm. Which was fabulous, since they were mates, but enjoying the visual feast laid out before him didn't answer a few vital questions.

A sudden mental itch stopped him in his tracks, and he tiptoed back to double-check if there was a bite mark on her anywhere. They hadn't bothered to crawl under the covers, the heat from their shifter bodies enough to keep them warm. That left every succulent inch of her exposed, and Shaun was suddenly curious about more than discovering if he'd already marked her.

Her smooth, chocolate-brown skin was unmarred by bruises, or any bite marks. The long elegant line of her neck revealed bare flawless flesh.

Why hadn't he marked her? He wanted a mate. Even staring at her now his interest in getting to know her all over again rose.

What was the better choice? Escape now and have a mature discussion once she woke wherein he would grovel and beg for forgiveness, or should he try to fake his way through, at least for a while?

He'd hate to be in the doghouse before he'd even had sex. Well, sex he could remember.

A low beeping noise sounded and Shaun scrambled back, searching for the source before the clatter woke his mystery mate.

Lying on the dresser was a slim cell phone, and he picked it up in time for the ringing to stop and a message to flash onto the screen. *Gemmita, call me.*

"Shaun?"

He spun, tucking his hands behind him. Shaun coughed lightly to cover the sound of the phone hitting the wooden surface of the dresser as he dropped it. His dark beauty had woken, curling those spectacular legs in as she sat up. She did naked very well.

*Gem.*

Relief flooded him. Okay, that was one thing back in the right spot in his memory banks. She'd asked him to call her Gem.

"Hey." He glanced around for a moment, looking for more clues.

She blinked. "You okay?"

"Sure. Of course. Why wouldn't I be?" Shaun leaned back casually on the dresser.

One of her perfectly arched brows rose. Then she smiled and patted the mattress beside her. "We should have that talk we didn't have last night."

*What?* He greeted her words like a small miracle. Shaun sauntered forward. Casually. That was going to be his catchword for the next however the hell long.

"Gem."

Her smile lit up, and when he sat next to her she snuggled in tight and lifted her lips to be kissed.

Shaun paused. What a strange situation. They'd already had sex, and here, this was what he would consider their first kiss. He took a deep breath, appreciating the way her scent made tiny alarms go off all over his body. Then he brushed their mouths together. Soft. Tender.

She gave a happy sigh, caressing his cheek gently a second before threading her fingers in his hair and pressing harder against him. Her mouth was open, her tongue darting out to tease his lips.

Her name was Gem, she was his mate, and she was delicious. Did he really need to know more?

It took a great deal of strength to pull away when what he wanted was to crawl over her and make love all morning. Maybe all day. Heck, he didn't have any true commitments until three days from now when he had a private booking.

"Shit." He'd be gone for a couple weeks at the least. Shaun smiled to reassure her, a puzzled expression crossing her face at his exclamation. "Yeah, we need to talk, because...oh man, there's a lot we need to figure out."

Gem wiggled back on the bed, and he swallowed hard. She sat perfectly straight, which meant her breasts were now staring him in... Well, he was staring at them.

Wolves might be okay with naked, but this was his mate, and he was freaking a little he wanted her so much. He stood and examined the room.

"What are you looking for?"

Shaun paced toward the bathroom. "Clothes, towels, the bed sheets. Something to cover you."

Gem laughed. "Am I that ugly?"

The connecting door to the next room was open, sunlight streaking across the floor to spotlight rather messy piles of abandoned clothing. He recognized one article and scooped it up, turning to toss his shirt to her. "Trust me, love. If you want to talk, I can't have you naked or the only talking will be our bodies."

"Then you'd better find something to wear, so I don't become overwhelmed with lust as well." She winked before turning to examine the shirt he'd tossed her. An adorable little frown appeared on her face as she wrinkled her nose and sniffed. Gem left his shirt on the bed as she headed to her suitcase and took out a long shimmery...thing. Shaun watched in fascination as she pulled it on, the floor-length garment wrapping her trim body in meters of mouthwateringly see-through fabric.

"I don't know if that's going to help the situation."

She sat in the corner chair, legs crossed at the ankle. The swath of layers around her hid enough his brain functioned. He stepped into his room and scrambled until he had managed to turn his jeans right side out and tug them on sans underwear, since that article of clothing seemed to have vanished altogether.

If they hadn't talked last night, maybe he wasn't as far up shit creek as he'd supposed. A moment's unease snuck in. While it was fairly normal for strangers to discover they were mates, he had never imagined the logistics of what having it happen to him would mean. Saying there was a lot for them to discuss was an understatement of massive proportions.

Shaun took a deep breath and hoped like hell whatever good karma he'd earned in his life to this point would somehow descend right about now.

He marched back into her room feeling somewhere between being ushered into paradise and being offered a long walk off a short plank.

# Chapter Six

Gem was sore in all the right places. The only thing that made her sad was the lack of a warm body snuggled against her. She'd been looking forward to waking in Shaun's arms and seeing what other mischief they could get up to. While she didn't have a ton of experience, sex with a mate was much better than anything she'd experienced before—she had so many things she wanted to try with him.

Shaun returned to her room and nabbed his shirt off the bed, snapping the wrinkled garment a few times before tugging it on and flopping down opposite her. Even rumpled and a total mess, he was all kinds of sexy. She imagined he'd look more impressive yet in a silk shirt. A pale blue would be spectacular against his skin.

"You come here often?" His delicious voice stroked her, and there was that smile again. The one that made her heart rate double.

She shook her head as she laughed. "My first trip north. You?"

Shaun rearranged the pillows against the headboard and leaned into them. "Born and bred in the Yukon. My family has been a part of the Takhini pack for generations. We have stories dating back to the gold rush. Of course, none of us hit it rich, but we did okay."

"Do you work for the pack?" She could already hear the questions her father would ask, so she'd better get those out of the way first.

"Nope—well, lately I've been giving Evan a hand and doing the bouncer thing in the bar, just to keep out of trouble." He paused and made a funny face.

*A bouncer.* Gem kept her smile firmly in place. Well, at least his position wasn't something that would lock him in the north. He could get a job in one of the local bars.

Or they could buy a bar for him if he wanted. There were many possibilities to consider.

Gem pulled her legs up and hugged them tight. "I'm not employed right now. Once I finish my degree, I hope to get a position with one of the family companies. Maybe working in environmental research for green products and controlling the impact of industry. It's a fascinating field."

"But you're here for the summer?" he asked.

"I'm here for a few weeks, yes."

Shaun frowned. He opened his mouth and paused. When he did speak, it was obvious he'd changed tangent.

"Anyway, I own an aviation company with a friend. Tad does less flying and more of the bookings these days because he's got a young family, and he's pretty busy with all his pack work. We've hired an additional pilot to help pick up the slack, and I do all the helicopter flights. We contract out to an adventure company called Maximum Exposure."

"You fly..." Gem adjusted her image of him as a red-necked, untrained brute, just a second before it hit her. "Maxwell's Silver Hammer."

"Right. You've heard of our company? That's cool."

"I've hired you."

Shaun sat upright. "The caribou trip? You? You're the insane scientist who wants to go into the bush for two weeks?"

"Insane?"

Shaun snorted. "Sorry, not you personally. It's just that almost every occasion in the past that we've had a southerner book flights into the backcountry, things have gone nutso. Statistically, you're a walking time bomb."

She wasn't sure when she'd crossed her arms in front of her, sitting even straighter than usual. His comments were not what she'd expected, not in terms of the trip or their relationship.

"I've contracted a perfectly acceptable research project, with all the background information completed. I simply need to gather the final hard data and report my findings."

His expression of disbelief hadn't budged. "You want to go chase caribou?"

"Yes."

"You."

The heat in the room kept rising, but no longer because she wanted to jump him. "Me. To complete a project for my undergrad studies."

"But *you*? Love, show me your hands."

She tugged them from under her robe and snapped them in his face. He took one and rested it in his palm. Like a knight of old, he kissed her.

Gem huffed. "This isn't the end of our discussion."

He shook his head, but didn't take his eyes off her fingers. He stroked them, long draws with his hand, his thumb on one side, the other four fingers rubbing and massaging. "So soft."

Shaun rotated her palm upward and touched his lips to the pulse point on her wrist. The echo of lust-filled pleasure from the previous night reverberated through her body. "Stop. Please."

Another kiss. "You don't want to go into the bush. These beautiful hands aren't the kind to handle the work."

Her rising passion was doused by a bucket of all-too-familiar discouragement. She yanked her hand free and rose to her feet.

"I am very capable of whatever it takes to complete this assignment. I'll have you know I practiced everything I needed for the wilderness part of the excursion." Gem stomped to the dresser, head held high. Of course, bare feet on carpet meant her heaviest treads didn't make much of an impact.

"Practiced? What did you practice? Getting lost in the scrub brush? Making a cat hole?" Shaun turned to follow her, his handsome face highlighted by a huge smile.

If he laughed, her response would involve pain on his part. She was so *so* sick of not being taken seriously, even if she had no idea what he was talking about.

What in the world had she done? Going off on such a wild hair and diving into bed with him before they had a chance to talk—all her lovely morning-after thoughts were well and truly trampled underfoot.

"Shaun, we've kind of gotten off topic. Maybe we should stick to background information for a bit longer, and we can worry about our work later."

He nodded slowly. "Right. Okay. Well, I'm the youngest of two kids. My sister mated a fellow a couple years ago, and they live in Fairbanks, Alaska. My mom and dad are part of the Takhini pack, but they aren't back from Florida yet."

"Florida?" That was her backyard. Almost. "Oh, right. Snowbirds?"

Shaun laughed. "Yeah, only they found a 55-plus community that's on the edge of a natural reserve, and the place is shifter-friendly. Most of the residents are either wolves or foxes, and once a week instead of bingo, they have tracking contests."

"We have mainly shifters on the grounds as well. Actually, all shifters. I didn't meet my first human until I was ten."

Shaun lost a bit of his smile. "Where do you live that you didn't meet a full human until you were that old? That's insane."

There was that word again. Gem chose to ignore the rude remark this time. "Our house is in southeastern Georgia close to Savannah. The estate borders a river and some woods, and there's a small community of residences around the perimeter. That's where most of the estate workers live."

"School? Didn't you go to a local school?"

Gem stared at him. "Of course I did. I just told you there was a community next to the estate. I went to grade and middle school there before attending a private school for upper grades."

"It's like you've been in a little shifter bubble your entire life. What about now? You said you're doing research for an undergrad degree. Which university? You've got to be attending campus somewhere."

A hint of embarrassment rose. "Well...no. I'm registered at Savannah, but most of my classes have been tutorials or home study. There's a full lab on the estate, and my classmates join me there for projects."

At the expression of absolute horror on his face, she crossed her arms in defense.

He shook his head in wonder. "Incredible. I didn't know this kind of situation existed."

"It's perfectly acceptable."

"You haven't been living in the real world." Shaun leaned closer, his gaze narrowing. "Hang on. Your classmates come to the estate? The prof as well?"

She nodded.

"What the hell kind of kickbacks does that take to arrange?"

*Kickbacks?* "What are you talking about? Daddy simply asked and they come. There was never any trouble. I always had tutors visit the house when I needed them."

"Wolves, right?"

"Usually."

"Because associating with humans was beneath you?"

Gem laughed. "Of course not. It was a safety issue. Do you know any US history? The natural lupine population was eradicated from Georgia during the 1960s. To this day residents can shoot wolves on sight without a permit."

His eyes widened in horror. "Holy shit. Really?"

Her amusement faded rapidly. "It isn't a great setting for a non-stable teen shifter to be out in public, which is why I assume my family organized private studies in the first place."

"And you still live there? I'd have thought all the shifters would have gotten the hell out."

"The estate has been our family's home for generations, and we don't want to abandon our heritage. We've adapted. Only it means that Daddy is more protective than I'd like. That's part of the reason I decided to do this trip. Spread my wings a little, and show that I'm capable."

Shaun fell silent. He strode to the window and threw open the curtains. Bright sunshine flooded the room. Gem caught herself fidgeting with her robe and deliberately folded her hands together, standing in a position that said relaxed, even though she was far from it.

The addictive sensation of his touch hadn't faded. The incredible awareness of having him inside her lingered, intimate and demanding. While the physical need to jump him remained, she wasn't at all happy with the way their conversation had progressed.

Shaun rotated, backlit by the sunshine. "What's your name?"

"I told you—"

"I can't remember your last name." He snapped the words.

She lifted her chin. "Jacobs."

His response was not what she expected. He buried his face in his hands for a second. "Holy fucking *hell*."

This time it wasn't a thrill of excitement that hit upon hearing his curse. "Shaun! Such language."

He gaped at her. "You're a Jacobs? Like the southern multibillionaire Jacobs who owes half the land in Georgia and—"

"That's not true."

Shaun collapsed back onto the foot of the bed. "Oh, sorry. Slight exaggeration on my part. Only a quarter of the state. You're a fucking heiress."

"Shaun. Enough swearing." She pulled herself upright with as much poise as possible, years of experience of dealing with dignitaries helping her deal with her mate. "There's no need for you to be vulgar. Yes, I'm a Jacobs, and we own a few properties and such. When we go back home, you can discuss with Daddy what part of the family business most interests you. With your background in aviation, you might like to take over one of the airlines at some point."

Gem trailed off. The expression on his face had shifted from disbelief to disgust.

"You expect me to move to Georgia?"

"Of course. Why wouldn't you? We're mates."

Shaun rose and stepped against her body. The desire to wrap herself around him was instant and strong, but she kept her hands in place, fingers gripped together tightly. He stared down, one finger stroking her cheek. He took a slow breath, as if calming himself. "Yes, we're mates. That means you can come and live with me. That's how this works. My sister met her mate, then she moved to be with him."

"And sometimes it works the other way. It makes more sense—"

He grabbed the back of her neck, his hand warm and gentle on her skin even as his words cut and stabbed. "I'm sorry, there's nothing that makes sense to me about abandoning my business, my life and my friends to go become a pampered boy toy for the Rockefellers of the wolf world. Not to mention moving somewhere I could be shot on sight—forget that shit."

"But I'm supposed to give up everything to come live with you?"

"It's where you belong." Shaun brushed his thumb over her cheek as he spoke.

Disappointment, deep and heartfelt slammed into her. Her mate was as controlling as her father, and frankly, she'd had more than enough of being a docile little lamb.

She wasn't about to give up the independence she'd worked so hard for over the past year. Maybe she appeared soft and fragile, but golly gee, she hadn't spent all that time training and learning to stand on her own just to toss it away to mate with a footloose drifter.

She caught his hand in hers, stilling the caress that was simultaneously making her body tremble and her heart break. "Then it's a good thing we didn't mark each other, isn't it? Because until we come to an agreement about how to deal with this situation, there will be no marking, understand?"

Gem slipped under his hand and snatched up her clothes, ignoring his protests as she stepped into the bathroom and firmly closed the door on his face.

Shaun spun his spoon between his fingers. Played with his coffee cup. Leaned back in his chair and rocked it precariously on two feet. He'd dressed and paced the room until Gem had basically ordered him to wait in the restaurant for her. It was either follow directions or break down the bathroom door, which she'd locked on him, and since he didn't think Evan would appreciate him smashing up the hotel, he'd taken his reluctant carcass away and left his mate alone.

As he sat pondering his future, he didn't know if he should run and hide, or go buy flowers.

"Careful. You break the chair, Evan will charge you to replace it. At least he always charges me."

A familiar teasing grin poked into Shaun's line of vision, and he caught himself a split second before tipping over onto his ass.

"TJ, what're you doing here?"

The lanky young man grabbed the chair next to him, pivoted it to face backwards, and sat, straddling the seat. "Pam's coming home today for a two-week stint. I'm picking her up at the airport, then we're doing the four-hour drive back to Haines. Granite Lake pack is holding a celebratory..."

He sniffed the air, and his eyes grew wide.

*Oh shit.* TJ had the best nose in the north. Shaun figured Gem's scent was all over him, and not only as a female he'd spent the night with for a bit of slap and tickle. He held up a hand. "I don't want to hear it."

As usual TJ ignored him. "Holy cow. Do I smell what I think I smell?"

"Shut it." Just what he didn't need. Love advice from someone nearly ten years his junior who until last year was best known for causing natural disasters everywhere he went. Didn't matter that he and TJ belonged to different packs, there was enough history between them Shaun should have been eager to share his news, but no. Fucking. Way.

His friend paused for a moment then shrugged. "Okay."

TJ motioned for the waitress, and she zipped over to pour him a coffee and top up Shaun's.

It was the coward's path. Shaun took an extra long time adding sugar and cream to his cup in an attempt to avoid having to talk. To justify why he was sitting here by himself when it would be clear to any wolf in the area that he had just found his mate.

The urge to blurt out something—to explain away what he didn't really understand himself—was so strong Shaun had to bite his lips.

For once, TJ seemed to take the hint and drop the subject.

"You heading to the hangar in Haines Junction soon? Tad had me go get the aircraft ready for the summer season." TJ grimaced. "The float plane was easy, but I don't know what the hell you left in the chopper the last time you flew her. There were like a million mice nesting in there."

"Sorry."

"You're worse than the pack kids. You know, when I dropped in at Tad and Missy's last week I nearly broke my neck, and it wasn't me being a klutz. Those kids have enough Lego to build a causeway to Russia. Plus, with the balls and stuffed shit there are times I think..."

Shaun pinched the bridge of his nose. Having TJ *not* ask about his mate was worse than having the discussion.

He gave up and scowled at the younger wolf. "Met her last night."

TJ thumped rapidly on the chair back in front of him to produce a drum roll. "Now we're getting somewhere. You work fast."

*Damn wolf genes.* "It wasn't my idea."

TJ gave him *the look.* "Believe me, I know about having choices taken out of your hands. You're a wolf, mating is never completely your decision." He glanced around before warning, "Just a heads-up. That excuse, *it wasn't my idea?* Like totally gets my ass kicked when I try to use it."

That was old news. Shaun had never let others get away with that wimpy whine before either, but he still fought the urge to groan. "She's not from around here."

TJ whistled, soft and low. "Hmm, that sucks. But, Shaun, while I bet the whole situation looks pretty impossible? Anything is doable. Pam's south for months at a time as she waits for her transfer to come through. And since having me move to Vancouver with her and bag groceries or pump gas is stupid when I'm needed up here... Yeah, the living-apart thing isn't fun, but for now it's the only solution."

Explaining to TJ what exactly about his mate made his skin itch when he didn't really know himself made this conversation impossible. "Well, let's just say we're working on figuring things out. By the way, you want to pass on a couple of messages to your brother and Tad for me?"

"Sure, what's up?"

"Tell Tad that I've got that flight to the north all taken care of, and let Keil know I'll be the one guiding the trip."

TJ frowned. "You want to take over the guiding as well as the flying? But if you've found your mate, I'm sure Tad can get someone else—"

"I've got it, okay?" Shaun snapped. TJ backed off, his hands raised in mock surrender. Shaun sighed. This emotional rollercoaster was turning him into a psychotic wreck. "My mate is the client, and there's no way I'm letting her go north without me? So I'll do the flight, guide her and everyone can be happy. The company, my mate...me. Hurrah. Happy happy happy."

He forced a grin.

TJ pulled a face. "Don't push it too hard, dude. I hear you. I mean, I hear more than you think." He checked his watch.

Shaun did the same, starting to worry if Gem was going to join him or if she had run for the hills after their little enlightening conversation. He'd been a total jerk. Never suspected the extent of an ass he could be, but it was obviously a ginormous one.

TJ finished his cup of coffee and slapped some money on the table. "I need to get going but whatever is bugging you, I suggest you get your head out of the sand quick. This isn't you. I've never heard you whine before in your life. Hell, usually you're the one telling everyone else to get their act together. Did you wake up this morning and make a shit list?"

Guilt smacked him like an avalanche. Yeah, he kinda sounded as if he'd made a list of everything he thought was fucked up and simply complained about them one after another. "It's not what I expected to be dealing with this week."

TJ shrugged as he rose to his feet. "That's reality. If everything ran according to a plan, life would be pretty boring. Finding your mate is an incredible gift. But even though we've got the freaky wolf genes making the decision for us, it's our human side that lets us work out the details. Just take it one step at a time, okay?"

Shaun stared at the younger man in shock. "When the hell did you grow up? You've never lectured anyone before." He'd certainly never been on the receiving end.

His friend's grin got wider. "Self-defense. My mate is a very stubborn woman. I've learned over the past nine months if I want something, I either need to sweet-talk her into seeing things my way or turn the logic way up."

Everything in him wanted to laugh at the thought of TJ using logic, but Shaun figured he was far more screwed at this point than TJ, so who was he to argue? "Fine. I get the message."

Already a couple steps away, TJ turned back. He winked at Shaun. "For what it's worth, I think you can handle this."

There was no time to throw anything at him before TJ waved and ducked out through the restaurant doors.

Shaun sat back down, slumping in his chair. Logic? He'd been using none of it, simply reacting. With his dick. His mouth, his attitude.

He had done the deed with his mate, and he couldn't freaking remember. Why in the hell had that happened? Then there was the whole overreacting thing. Memories flashed of being a teenager and deliberately picking fights with his parents.

His stomach grumbled, and he checked his watch again. If Gem didn't show up soon he was going back to the room to haul her ass out for breakfast even if he had to remove the hinges—

Shock hit upside the head.

Shame.

*Holy shit.* He couldn't turn it off. Even sitting here he was thinking like a Neanderthal. As if that was the way to get the princess to do anything. She was his *mate.* He might not have marked her, but he was damn well not going to give her up.

He dropped his head into his hands, plotting as hard as he could. Okay, if he'd recited a list to TJ about everything wrong between him and Gem, maybe he needed to make that list again, and use some of *his* sweet-talking ability and keen logic to improve the situation. There were a lot of ways to accomplish goals, and one sure way was for the other person to offer you exactly what you wanted.

Well, maybe somewhere in the next day or two he'd figure out what exactly it was that he wanted. Because right now, he had absolutely no idea, other than his plans had to include her.

The doors to the restaurant opened again, and this time instead of TJ's ugly mug it was *her.* Pristine and perfect, dressed in a suit jacket with a matching knee-length skirt. Small heels on her shoes, dark hair pulled back to lie in immaculate sweeps over her shoulders. Shaun rose to his feet instinctively, and the frown on her face smoothed away.

Gem stepped slowly toward him, and he held out his hand.

"Ready for breakfast?" he asked. Polite. Almost formal. Shaun grit his teeth at how weird it felt to try and impress a female this way.

"Starving." He held her chair, then waved down the waitress. Gem adjusted her place setting before looking up from under lowered eyelashes to smile hesitantly at him. "I seemed to have burned off a few extra calories last night."

*Sweet mercy.* He licked his lips and discarded the first half-dozen responses that shot to mind—all of them far too dirty to voice.

Gem accepted a menu and examined it closely, giving him more time to stare in fascination at what fate had laid in his path. Mentally, he scrambled to organize the list—the *winning Gem over* list.

Number one. She was from the south, he loved the north. That was the biggest and most obvious barrier between them. Somehow he had to convince her that where she wanted to be was here. The beauty of the north was unlike anywhere else in the world, especially for wolves. Being able to enjoy the freedom of running through wide open spaces—he bet she'd never gotten to experience anything like that down south—not with the freaky "no wolves in Georgia" deterrent.

The waitress came by to take their orders and top up his coffee. Gem lifted her cup and took a long appreciative sniff. "Smells delicious."

"Midnight Sun brewing company. Locally owned, and they roast the beans right here in Whitehorse. We've also got one of the pack who is a gourmet chef working the Moonshine Inn. You won't find better in the fanciest restaurant elsewhere."

"Really? How wonderful." Gem took a slow sip and Shaun looked around helplessly for puppies to pet or something equally awe-inspiring. Five minutes into the meal, and he was reduced to boasting about the social graces of the north? *Gag.*

Still, desperate times, desperate measures.

While they waited for their order to arrive, Gem shared about her trip north the previous day. Even as she spoke, Shaun nodded absently and mentally scrambled through his foggy memory banks. She had mentioned something vital this morning. Something about...spreading her wings and trying new things.

She'd been protected—really, *really* sheltered up to this point in her life. Although the fact concerned him and made all his own protective instincts rev up to high, her wanting to experience a freer life could work right into his game plan. He would show her around, but allow her space. He totally understood that need.

Gem continued to examine the restaurant as if fascinated. It allowed him time to add *give Gem breathing room* to his list.

The biggest worry he had right now was her crazy trip to the North Country.

Over the years, most of the bookings he'd flown that had turned out disastrous involved members of the research community. What they thought was adequate preparation in the lab had been nowhere near what was needed in the bush. The only way Gem could get her information would involve a lot more hands-on activity than helicopter fly-bys. They would have to hike and camp on the actual terrain.

Their breakfast arrived, and Gem smiled sweetly at the waitress before dipping into her food. Shaun tried to picture her in the middle of his usual going-back-to-the-land-to-relax situation, and couldn't. Simply couldn't. The delicate aura surrounding her turned him on, then wrapped him in knots of fear. What if she hated the trip? He came out of his intense concentration to catch her staring.

She reached across the table to touch his hand. "Is everything all right?"

Shaun nodded rapidly. "Fine, just fine. Wonderful."

"You're frowning."

Because he'd imagined her taking one look at the primitive campsite they'd be living in for days and running as fast as her pretty little shoes could take her, as far away from him as possible.

He scrambled for some logical excuse. "Too much coffee. I should switch to decaf. Orange juice?" He offered his glass and her expression smoothed again.

Somehow he had to convince her there was another way to finish her project without subjecting her to full-out wilderness in her first days up north. It really would be better for them all if she decided to cancel the trip. He didn't need her to get so discouraged she turned and ran south before she'd had time to truly fall in love.

With both him and the land.

# Chapter Seven

Gem made sure the breakfast conversation stuck to light, non-*them* related issues. They might have far too many details to figure out, but based on how fabulous their earlier discussion had gone, she didn't want to be fighting indigestion as well as anger for the rest of the day.

Instead she played the ultimate diplomat. If there was one thing her years acting as her father's hostess had taught her, it was how to talk about absolutely anything, with anyone, and say nothing.

If only she didn't keep losing her concentration every time their elbows bumped. Or when their fingers touched as he passed her the salt. When he'd offered her a taste of his fresh-squeezed orange juice, she'd nearly had heart palpitations. Even sharing a glass with him was far too intimate.

Finally, Shaun stared at her over his empty plate. "Had enough?"

She dabbed her mouth with her napkin and nodded. "That was delicious, thank you."

He led her back toward their rooms. She paused in the foyer. "I know the official sightseeing wasn't suppose to begin until we leave Whitehorse, but would you be interested in showing me around?"

His grin was mesmerizing. "I would love to be your guide.

Put yourself entirely into my hands."

*Into his hands.* The coals in her belly fanned to high heat, and she forced herself to ignore them. Not now. They had already established they could have sex. Hot sex. Melt-the-sheets sex.

Could they go for a walk without starting another argument?

"I'd like that." She paused again. "I should change."

He eyed her, admiration clear. "I don't want you to change a thing."

That wasn't what it had sounded like before, but she'd take the statement at face value. "Thank you."

Shaun offered his hand and she accepted it, her fingers tingling where they made contact. He led her out the front doors to where the sun was already high overhead. A lingering coolness hung in the air as the breeze flowed over the river.

It was peaceful and serene—walking quiet streets with hints of brilliant green showing everywhere. Considering it was June and she'd seen Savannah bloom back in March and April, to realize it was only spring here was another reminder of just how far away from home she was. He squeezed her hand and pointed to a nest, the white head of a bald eagle peeking over the edge.

She was loath to break their companionable silence, but they had to begin the discussions sometime. "Do you live right in Whitehorse?"

Shaun laughed. "That's a tough question. When I'm not working tourist flights or shipping supplies, yes, I live here in town in the pack house. I also have an apartment in Haines Junction—that's where we store the planes."

"Two places?"

"Yeah, means less time on the road. In the summer, my partner and I fly most of the bookings for Maximum Exposure Wilderness Expeditions. Tad's Alpha and brother-in-law owns that company. Then in the dead of winter, I chopper medical and emergency supplies to Old Crow and other people in remote areas who get isolated in the cold season."

They'd arrived at a walkway that paralleled the river. With a gentle pressure on her hand, he held her back for a moment, pointing across to where a section of lingering ice had just broken loose from the bank. The minute iceberg drifted past them, slowly spiraling on the lazy current of the wide river.

Her mate wasn't simply a shiftless bum after all. Something inside warmed that had nothing to do with her wolf and the way it kept nudging her to touch him. "That sounds like a very noble occupation."

The mischievous grin was back, the dark centers of his eyes like magnets, catching her and refusing to let her go. "Yeah. And the pay is good too. Additional benefits because of the danger, you know."

One word nabbed her attention. "Danger?"

He grunted lightly. "If you have a mechanical breakdown that far back in the bush, and you don't find shelter quick, you can pretty much kiss your ass goodbye."

Gem deliberately ignored his swearing. "But you're a wolf, so that reduces some of the risk."

"Even wolves can freeze when it's minus sixty, love."

In spite of the sun's warmth, Gem shivered. "The estate stays above freezing all winter, and for much of the year, flowers bloom everywhere over the grounds. There's a pool for the hot summer days as well, but my favourite thing has always been going to the beach."

"Really?" His surprise was genuine. "You..."

She waited.

He stopped at the base of a bridge. "I was going to say you don't strike me as the beach type."

Gem had to give him that one. "I don't enjoy getting sand everywhere, but there's something about the waves I love. And how big and free the ocean is—it moves me."

"Hmm." Shaun stared at her for a moment, then gestured over the bridge. "Want to see the fish ladder?"

"I'd love to." She'd read about it. Checked the online information. Getting to see it in person—even better. That's what she needed more of. To expand what she'd only witnessed in books and research into life experiences.

Shaun caught her hand again and tugged her across the gently curved footbridge. "Building the hydro-dam caused Miles Canyon to flood and back up to form Schwatka Lake. Of course the dam not only stopped the water, it blocked the salmon from their traditional spawning grounds, and so the city installed the ladder."

He took her to the viewing house, and they peered through the glass at the running water. The slope of the wooden trough appeared gentle enough the fish would be able to fight the current and swim the extension waterway all the way from the base of the falls to the top of the dam.

"There's nothing here now, but in the fall the salmon arrive by the thousands, and the fish and wildlife dudes count them as they go up the chute." Shaun hopped over the security fence to dig in a wooden box. He picked up a plastic salmon and displayed it to her. "They're about this size by the time they get here."

Gem glanced around, hoping she wouldn't spot anyone official coming to clap them in irons. "Put it down. Oh, dear."

"You want to touch it?"

She must have looked like Spock. She felt her one brow rise way, way up in the air. "Why?"

He dropped the plastic prop back in the box, grinning the entire time.

Then he hauled her up the hill to what he called the best viewpoint in town. Shaun pointed out landmark buildings, shared history tidbits and some of his own personal escapades. Somehow his arm snuck around her waist without her even noticing. Leaning into his side felt very right. Brand new and at the same time as if she was coming home.

Maybe...this relationship wasn't going to be as difficult as she had first feared.

An hour later, they were back on Main Street, strolling past all those quaint little places she'd seen on the drive in. The scent of coffee in the air nearly made her mouth hang open.

"Could we stop for a moment?"

Shaun smiled his agreement. "How about lunch?"

He guided her through a massive set of wood doors, and warm air laced with fresh-baked bread filled her nostrils, followed by another familiar scent.

"Ho there. Gather your libations and join us." In the corner of the shop, someone waved a hand. Evan, accompanied by the human woman from the hotel.

Gem and Shaun both hung back for a second. On her part, it was because of the sudden realization Evan would know they had mated. The wide smile on the Alpha's face increased her suspicions. This was his "figure it out in the morning" solution?

She wasn't sure if she should hit him or hug him.

Shaun bumped her hip with his. "I'll grab us grub, okay? You go ahead and sit down."

He vanished back to the pickup counter before she could

protest.

Fine. Gem stepped forward boldly, accepting the seat Evan graciously held for her. At least not all the northern wolves were without manners.

Just hers. *Heavy sigh.*

"Caro, have you met Gemmita? She's up north to do some research. Gemmita, this is Caroline. Head of the admin department at the Moonshine Inn and my right-hand man." Evan winked. "So to speak."

Gem nodded politely. "We met at the hotel. Nice to see you again."

Evan leaned on his elbows and tilted his head toward Shaun. "So. You and him mates?"

Utter shock at him discussing such a thing in front of a human froze her tongue.

She must have unwittingly made a face because Caroline patted her hand. "It's okay. I know about wolves. My stepdad and stepsiblings are all shifters."

"Really? That's very unusual. I mean, it's uncommon down in Georgia." Astonishment was followed by a flash of insight.

When she'd set out on this excursion, she'd had no intention of being entrenched in wolf society. Yet in less than a day she'd fallen back into the familiar pattern of feeling comfortable around pack, simply because they were pack. The idea of sitting and talking with a human had made her hesitate at the door almost as much as anticipating Evan's reaction to her and Shaun's mating.

Comprehension allowed her to let the curiosity she felt rise.

She'd never been in this position before, having someone fully human she could discuss wolves with. Caroline must have a million experiences to share. With one smooth swipe, some of

Gem's unvoiced concerns fell away. After years of dealing with people during formal events with her father, she knew she was more than capable of having polite conversation in public without anyone holding her hand.

Moreover, she had a lot of other skills that would be needed over the next weeks—not just the ones she'd practiced in the lab, but ones to let her take care of herself. Being helpless wasn't part of her plan for this trip—she didn't want to be coddled by anyone. Not by her father, not by her mate.

Happiness accompanied by a tiny bit of pride warmed her, and Gem turned to pepper Caroline with questions.


Evan sat and watched the women, contentment rising as he sipped his drink. Gemmita and Shaun's mating, although they were a bit of an odd couple, didn't concern him much. The tension between them was thick enough to cut right now, but that was to be expected. Knowing how strong Shaun was and having experienced a taste of Gemmita's power the previous night, it was inevitable the two of them would take some time to find a point of balance.

His own future seemed far more uncertain.

Caroline had surprised him that morning, but after a couple hours of thinking through her proposition, he had to admit there was merit in it. Being distracted by the single ladies jostling for position had delayed his actual plans. A temporary moratorium on his solo-ness could help him make some important progress in amalgamating the two Whitehorse packs—which had been his goal since he had taken control of Takhini barely a year ago.

Would Caroline really be able to handle the rest of the pack? She had a way with people, evidenced by her skills at the hotel, but wolves were a cocky bunch. And they liked to get physical when they were uncertain or happy or... Hell, wolves just liked to get physical.

He let his gaze slip over her curves. More importantly, had she thought through what moving in with him implied? If the ploy was going to work, it wasn't just her presence in his house he'd require. The entire crew would know if they were sleeping together or not.

Besides, while he'd love to have the ladies off his tail, he didn't relish the idea of being celibate. Not one little bit.

Shaun approached, tray piled high with food and drink. Evan changed his position, deliberately moving closer to Caroline. Then he oh-so-casually stretched his arm along the back of her chair.

Instantly, her scent picked up like usual. Sexual arousal— spicy and invigorating. Yeah, he'd always known she was attracted to him physically. He took another deep breath, savouring her reaction and considering again if he should accept her offer.

"When will you be heading out to do your study?" Caroline didn't jerk away as he dropped his fingers onto her shoulder, stroking her almost absently.

Gem accepted a drink from Shaun and turned back to answer Caroline. "I had thought the flight was to leave on Saturday, but I guess since Shaun is my pilot and guide, he can tell you better than I can."

"Yeah, well..." Shaun twisted in his chair. "About that. We need to discuss some specifics. There are a few complications."

Her whole body tightened. "Really? Doesn't seem that complicated to me. I hired you to fly me to Dawson and then farther north. Did you need more time to arrange tickets or file for permission or something? I assumed you'd have everything all in place since I prepaid a deposit. I seem to remember receiving confirmation that the trip was a go."

Shaun wiggled like a two year old, and Evan hid his grin. The irresponsible devil had something on his mind, and for the first time in history, he wasn't simply spitting out everything without a thought. Maybe this mate business would be what it took to make Shaun live up to his full potential.

Evan watched the impending fireworks with interest, even as he played with the back of Caroline's neck, caressing her skin, enjoying himself immensely.

She glanced at him, but he ignored the question on her face. Their conversation would come after the two lovebirds in front of them either spontaneously combusted or settled down.

Shaun nodded slowly. "I have the flights arranged, only the timing isn't right for a direct trip. It's best if we head up to Dawson City on Saturday and spend some time there looking around. We have to wait for word that the herd has moved past the Porcupine River before we can leave."

A sharp acknowledgement from Gem. "I mentioned that in my request—I knew there would be matters of timing to deal with. That's why the sightseeing tour was added in. I did research, you know."

"Yes, but—" Shaun slammed his mouth shut.

Evan twisted in his seat, tempted to bury his face in Caroline's neck to be able to let out a laugh. Shaun's newfound self-control was extraordinary, although the sight was the funniest thing Evan had seen. How to bell a wolf? Bring in a Gem.

"But what? Of course, I'll pay for your accommodations while we're waiting in Dawson. Simply part of the research costs." Gem offered a scone to Caroline, ignoring the wolf at her side who looked as if he was about to burst out foaming at the mouth.

"I don't need you to pay. In fact, we'll be refunding your deposit." Shaun stared at her.

"I don't think that's wise. Your business partner has young children. I'm sure they need to eat. I'll pay as usual."

"You're my mate, you're not paying."

"I can afford it, I'm paying."

They glared at each other for a second before Gem coughed lightly and once again turned to speak to Caroline.

Shaun interrupted. "Look, fine. You can pay the cost of the trip, but not the extra. It's my time, I'm donating it to you."

Gem blinked. "Thank you."

Shaun sat back, content.

"...but no," she continued. "I want to do this, and I'm going to do this. On my own, without being catered to by my father or my mate or anyone else who thinks they have a piece of control over me."

Heat flushed Shaun's face. "That makes no sense at all. Why not let me help—"

She stood. "Because you don't get it. I don't need help right now. I don't want help right now. I assume you have to go...somewhere to pick up the helicopter. My initial papers said you'd meet me at the Whitehorse airport on Saturday at noon. I will see you there at that time."

"But th-th-that's..."

Gem ignored the stuttering Shaun, nodding instead at Evan and Caroline. "Thank you for the lovely visit. Caroline, perhaps we could meet for dinner tonight? You know where I'm staying."

Then she lifted her chin and calmly stepped away from the table, leaving a stunned Shaun in her wake. He watched her walk a few paces before leaping to his feet.

"Shaun," Evan warned. "You might want to give her a little space to cool off."

His friend turned back in the middle of the room, the most pleased expression on his face. "Are you kidding? She's got a freaking backbone. I love it!"

Evan shrugged. "Your funeral, man."

Shaun disappeared out the door, running past the shop windows in his attempt to catch up with Gem.

The shoulder under his hand wiggled, and Evan glanced up to see Caroline shaking with silent laughter. "What's with you?"

She shook her head. "I don't think you can understand exactly how entertaining you wolves are when you're all hormone-driven with your mate thingy. I've never seen Shaun act like that before."

Evan laughed. "Yeah, well, somewhere they'll come to a solution. I hope. And about time too, for Shaun at least."

Caroline offered him one of the muffins from the table, and he placed it on his plate. She did know enough about wolves to deal with a lot of the shit that would go down if he accepted her offer.

But was she strong enough? To deal with the pack and handle him?

*Should I? Shouldn't I?*

Why the hell not?

She stopped in the middle of buttering her muffin. "Why are you staring at me like that?"

"Because your offer this morning is intriguing, and I'm going to say yes—on one condition."

Her eyes widened to the size of silver dollars. "One condition? What's that?"

He leaned back in his chair, gesturing to the empty seats

on the opposite side of the table. "Just like they need to work out a few things, we have to as well. You do know that if you move in, you'll be sleeping in my bed."

Not only were her eyes wide, but her jaw dropped open. "Oh shit, I forgot—"

"Because we're obviously not mates, and none of the pack will believe we're a real partnership if we're not having sex. So straight up, you okay with that?"

"With having sex with you?"

Damn, she was cute when she blushed. "Sex. Lots of it, too."

Then she snorted, and his ego got a little bruised. "Oh yes, the legendary wolfish sex drive. It's okay, Evan, I think I can handle anything you want to dish out. Only I'm not doing kinky things with you when you're in your wolf form. I draw the line at that."

*Ick.* "Of course not."

She straightened up, all business-like. "So, is that it? The condition is I agree to sleep with you?"

"Sleep, screw, fuck, roll in the—"

She slapped his arm. "Enough, I get it. Fine. Done. It might kill me, but for the sake of the hotel, I'll make the sacrifice."

He examined her closely to see if she was yanking his leg or not. *Damn human sense of humour.* "That's the first part of the condition."

Caroline laughed. "If there's another part, then you don't have one condition. You have two." She waved at him. "Go on."

"You have to claim me in front of the pack."

The way all the colour drained from her face was enough to let him know she understood exactly what he'd demanded.

"I claim you?" she forced out, low and hesitant.

*Hmmm.* "Did you think you could just move in and we'd announce it? Sweetie, this is pack. You can either deal with them, or you can't. What's it going to be?"

She stared out the window for a moment. He examined her smooth skin. Was he crazy for hoping she'd have the guts to go through with it?

When Caroline turned back to face him she had bright red spots on her cheeks, and a determined expression in her eyes. "Fine. When the time is right. I'm agreed."

She held out her hand and he took it. One firm shake later, they both let go and stared at each other.

Then she calmly returned to her muffin, asking about an order he'd suggested for the hotel. Business as usual.

Evan enjoyed the rest of his breakfast. Shaun was headed into his own personal wilderness with Gem, and here he was, also venturing into new territory. He looked forward to the next stage of the adventure.

# Part Two

There's nothing gained by whining,
  and you're not that kind of stuff;
You're a fighter from way back when,
  and you won't take a rebuff;
Your trouble is that you don't know
  when you have had enough—
Don't give in.
If Fate should down you, just get up and take another cuff;
You may bank on it that there is no philosophy like bluff,
And grin.

*"Grin"—Robert Service*

# Chapter Eight

She was as punctual as he expected. Shaun loaded her equipment and bags into the cargo section and completed his last-minute checks before returning to the airport hangar to escort her to the helicopter. Whitehorse was small enough he got to care for everything himself. The next commercial plane wasn't due in or out for over two hours, so there was no need to rush.

The sensation of panic haunting him had more to do with knowing that somehow in the next two weeks he had to make her fall in love with him, and prevent her from killing herself in the bush. Bloody tangled mess he'd gotten into.

She lit up the area with her smile as he approached the gate. "Shaun."

Damn, she was gorgeous. The urge to scoop her up and toss her into the back of the helicopter to ravish her was strong. His wolf was beyond pissed at him, for allowing them to be separated for the past three days.

He ignored her outstretched hands to pull her tight to his body and take a deep breath of her sweet scent. That was all it took—his wolf calmed in a flash.

"I missed you," he confessed.

She returned his embrace, the heat of her torso melding with his, and he couldn't let go. Her slight weight as she relaxed against him comforted the ache, then stirred the ashes. "I missed you as well."

She lifted her mouth and he eagerly accepted her lips.

*Public place, man.* It took a ton of energy to keep himself from consuming her like a bag of cotton candy. Instead, he gave her a gentle kiss. Maybe a little too gentle. He leaned away, and she grabbed his head, holding on to him and increasing the greeting to something on a higher-fire warning.

Hello, she tasted good.

They were both slightly breathless by the time they drew apart.

He finally noticed what she was wearing. "Sweet—like the boots."

Gem lifted a foot and displayed her hikers. "All broken in and everything. I've been walking around Whitehorse for the past two days to make sure I'm ready."

Two days? Shaun didn't have the heart to warn her that wasn't nearly enough time. "Awesome! Shall we go?"

She accepted his elbow and they made their way to the chopper. He dawdled over strapping her in, enjoying having his hands on her body again, even if she was buried under a bulky shirt and thick cotton pants. He liked her in those pants, liked the way they hugged her curves. For one terrible second the image of her wandering Whitehorse alone—and all the guys who got to see her in said pants—flashed into his brain and his temper flared.

*Cool. Keep it cool.*

"Did you enjoy your time in Whitehorse? Sorry I had to leave you, but there were things to do at the hangar before I could be ready for the trip."

Her smile dazzled him. "No problem—it was just wonderful.

Caroline and I did an aerobics class at the Canada Games Centre, then I went out to dinner with her at the Klondike Rib and Salmon and we ate with our fingers. It was so exciting."

Her enthusiastic descriptions helped the final preflight prep pass in a blur. He gave her a headset, taught her how to use the microphone to ask questions. Her obvious delight continued as he shared information about the landscape passing under them, but for the most part she simply leaned against the window and took it in. Fascination painted her face as he followed the Yukon River, the many tributaries trickling into the main waterway littered with small-claim shanties, even after all this time.

It was a sight that had always mesmerized him. He could only hope her thoughts were as positive as his, and that she wasn't aware how increasingly remote they were becoming.

"Do you have any idea yet how long a layover we'll have in Dawson?" she asked.

Shaun pulled himself back from his mental ramblings. "Looks like a week at the most. The herd is moving late this year."

"I checked the websites, but the data wasn't up to date." She pointed out the front window at a pair of moose darting into the bush at their approach.

"The radio-collar program the government set up gathers great information, but when they had a real-time website posting, the data was accessible to everyone. Including hunters, who then used it to plan their expeditions. Turns out the conservationists were unintentionally broadcasting the exact location of individual animals."

Gem shook her head in disgust. "That's terrible."

Shaun shrugged. "Hey, people use the resources offered. I don't agree with the hunters using the system, but I understand why they did. So the website is now on a time delay."

"How are you getting your information, then?" Gem placed her fingers on his arm, and the contact did wonderful wiggly things to his system.

He smiled. "I have my sources."

Her laughter danced over his ears. "Of course you do."

The admiration she displayed cheered him inside. *That's what he wanted more of*—that look in her eyes, that sweet smile on her lips—all for him. Somehow he had to maintain whatever was causing it, because making her happy was like a drug pouring back into his own system. "Local packs have always shared information to keep their territories as peaceful as possible. There's a wolf pack in Dawson, and at least a dozen more in the outlying communities of the north. Each one a little more remote, a little less civilized in some ways. I've gained contacts with them during my years of flying."

He glanced at her face. She remained enamored with the landscape, staring in fascination, and that was a fabulous start. Now he had to figure out how to make the time in Dawson memorable. And something outside the bedroom, although please to high heaven, could they have some time in the bedroom?

They still hadn't had sex. Not as far as he could remember.

The hours it took to get to Dawson seemed to pass in a few seconds. Just breathing her scent on the air made him ecstatic. Even though arriving meant they were that much closer to a fight, because another argument was inevitable. Their time in Dawson as they waited would involve mainly sightseeing. No problem there, but the next stage of the adventure, when the research began? Her plans needed to be adjusted, and somehow he didn't think she would take the news with a happy smile, not after the hell she gave him back at the coffee shop.

Landing at Dawson and arranging temporary storage for the chopper didn't take very long, and soon enough they were in a cab en route to their overnight stop. The streets were far busier than he ever remembered seeing before.

Arriving at the hotel threw all their positive travel mojo out the window.

Shaun eyed the man behind the counter and debated how he'd taste roasted. "What do you mean, cancelled? I had those rooms on a guaranteed reservation."

"I'm sorry, sir. I agree, the booking mistake is completely our error. Let me see what I can arrange for you instead." The clerk typed rapidly, his gaze frantic as he studied the computer screens. Shaun glanced over at Gem who sat behind him in the foyer, people watching. The expression of delight on her face intrigued him.

He wasn't sure if all the things she found captivating choked him up because he was shocked at her naivety, or because her enthusiasm made him realize he'd spent so much of his life not really noticing what was going on around him. Kind of like living in a constant state of "whatever".

"Sir? Unfortunately there are limited room choices left."

"We'll take anything you've got." Hang on. Back when they didn't know it was his mate he was ferrying, they had booked two rooms. "Oh, and one room is all we need."

Genuine relief covered the clerk's face. "Thank you for being so understanding. There's been a flood of visitors into town in the past couple days, and the extra bookings are making it difficult to do any shuffling."

"Convention?" Shaun asked.

The clerk shook his head. "Nothing in the Chamber of

Commerce notes or at the regular convention centre. But it's crazy. I suggest if you'd like to eat out you make reservations early."

Shaun accepted the key card and went to collect Gem. She stared at him from under her lashes as they waited in the elevator. When she licked her lips, his groin tightened.

*Oh please, oh please, oh please.*

He held the door for her, watching her ass with longing as she stepped past him. She turned and examined the room. There was that expression on her face again. The one that said she thought he was almost, but maybe not quite, out of his mind. He took a quick peek past her shoulder to try and spot what was wrong. This hotel wasn't the fanciest place in town— he hadn't wanted to go overboard in trying to impress her. The room was neat and tidy, sunshine streaming in the window.

"Two beds?"

Hope rose in a rush. It wasn't the lack of fancy amenities that had caught her attention. "There's some kind of convention in town and everything else was booked solid."

"I see." She slipped to the far bed and sat on the edge of the mattress, staring around the room before fixing her inquisitive gaze on him. "Well—what's first on the sightseeing agenda?"

Shaun pushed down the desire to suggest there was nothing he'd like to see more than her naked and waiting on that bed. "So much to do, so little time to do it in. Come on, let's paint the town red."

Bodies crowded the boardwalks. Far more hulking male bodies than she'd expected, and Gem was glad of Shaun's solid frame by her side. "Does it seem as if there's an awful lot of shifters around?" she asked, leaning to whisper in his ear.

"You'll find more shifters in general in the north. Living up here is safer, for one thing, and we all enjoy the open spaces. Gives us room to let our animal sides run when they want." Shaun pointed down the street. "Bears, wolves, cougars. Yeah, there is a huge variety of shifters here. Not as much as in Chicken, but—"

"Chicken?"

He led her into an old-fashioned theater. "That's a town just over the border in Alaska. Shifters-only for some strange reason. The original founders wanted to call the place Ptarmigan after the flocks of local birds, but no one could spell the word properly, so..."

"Chicken."

"Yup."

She laughed, then got distracted by the shimmering lights reflecting off the walls.

There was a stage at one end, noisy casino machines along the other. The center of the room was filled with tables, mostly occupied. Shaun urged her toward a couple empty seats, his fingers warm around hers. He gestured with his free hand.

"Welcome to Diamond Tooth Gertie's. The theater's been revamped. They did a great job of bringing her back to life like in her heyday."

Gem didn't know where to look next, everything was so fascinating. Turn-of-the-century fixtures, honky-tonk music. Waiters and waitresses in costumed garb. "Oh, her costume has a bustle. I have a dress like that."

Shaun plopped into a chair. "Really?"

She stood for a moment longer, and he bounced up like a yoyo.

"Shit, sorry." He held her chair as she sat, and she bit her lips to hide her smile. He was trying. That counted for something.

That counted for a lot.

Then the floorshow started, and she got lost in the narration. History filled her mind, more than just the disconnected bits of information she'd read over the years. The actors on the stage took her back and immersed her in the gold rush. In the daily struggles the Klondikers faced as they fought for survival in the wilds and scratched out a living from an uncertain future.

Gem found herself clinging to Shaun's hand as the tales unfolded.

When the curtain fell, she applauded as loudly as anyone in the room, strangely touched. It wasn't just the remembrance of people who had died long ago, but a sensation of something else. There were so many possibilities in her own future, so much more for her to experience.

His lips brushed her cheek. "Come, let's walk."

Outside, the sky was still daylight bright, the hills around them clear and the air fresh. Even at this time of night, the crush of people remained overwhelming. They ducked and dodged a constant stream of bodies, and the contentment she'd felt after the show slipped away. This wasn't what she wanted.

She'd enjoyed the flight to Dawson, and the attention Shaun had paid her. The respect he'd given in agreeing to her terms—letting her remain on her own in Whitehorse for three days... Well, she hadn't really let him do anything *but* agree with her, if she was honest. Still, exploring their relationship was what they needed now, not fighting a swarming mass of humanity and shifters, crowding and bumping into their space.

"Can we get away from this?" She ducked an errant elbow, and Shaun curled himself around her a little tighter.

"Back to the room?"

Their room. "That would be...lovely."

They stared at each other for a moment, and she wondered if all he could picture—like her—were the beds waiting for them at the hotel.

She'd felt some guilt for walking out on him at the restaurant the other day. And when he had caught up, she'd used all her strength to insist her decision was final. It had taken another ten minutes before she managed to get back to her room, forcing him to leave before she changed her mind.

Her wolf was very put out with her.

Shaun didn't seem to understand why she needed to do this trip. Yes, things had dramatically changed when they'd discovered each other. It didn't mean she was willing to abandon what she wanted to accomplish. If anything, it made her goals even more important.

She didn't want to be a weak person, not for him. And the way she'd been going was being weak. Depending completely on others' opinions and following the paths they planned for her— that was wrong. Plus, she didn't need another older man in her life making all the decisions. One father was enough. Shaun had to see her as his equal, or this partnership of theirs was going to go nowhere fast.

That didn't mean she didn't want him.

The crowds thinned by the time they reached the hotel, all the traffic on the street headed the opposite direction.

"It's a madhouse out there." Shaun pushed through the door then froze. "Fuck it. Sorry."

She gave him a wry smile. "Shaun, I won't knee you in the groin if you occasionally forget to open the door for me. I can handle doors."

He grinned sheepishly. "Good, because I totally want to keep my groin un-kneed."

She flushed. Thinking about that portion of his anatomy made taking their time to stroll to the elevators difficult. He leaned past her to press the call button, and his scent filled her nostrils. Made her mouth water and her knees quiver.

Suddenly, having been apart for a few nights seemed like the most insane—*there was that word again*—thing. And this time, it *was* her fault.

Two other couples joined them in the small compartment. Shaun stepped in front of her, as if to guard her. A terribly naughty thought popped into her mind, and as the doors clicked shut, she grabbed a handful of his shirt and tugged upward, hard. He stiffened, but didn't move as she slipped her hand under his T-shirt and let her fingers roam over his warm skin.

Oh dear, she was getting turned on just touching his back. Touching his side. Firm edges to the muscles, the swoop of his waist lined by the cut of his obliques. The elevator stopped and one couple left, opening more room. Rather than shifting away, Gem stuck to his side, sneaking her hand around to his abdomen. Under her fingers, his muscles quivered as she stroked the ridges of his six-pack. She watched his throat move as he swallowed hard, changing her touch to play with the faint dusting of hair lower down. The intriguing trail disappeared into where his shirt remained tucked into his pants in the front, and Gem longed to be able to dip her hand under the waistband.

The elevator door dinged, and she withdrew her hand quickly, dragging her fingernails lightly over his skin. Leaving her mark on his body.

She wanted her mate.

The door slid shut, and he whirled on her, his eyes more

feral than human. "You playing games?"

She shook her head, mouth gone dry. "No games. I want you."

The elevator couldn't open fast enough for either of them.


When he dropped the plastic card for the third time, Shaun was tempted to kick the door down. Gem scooped up the key, slammed it into place and shoved the door open all in one motion. She grabbed him by the back of his belt and yanked him in after her, finishing the job of stripping his shirt away rather handily.

"Your bed or mine?" She mouthed the words against his neck. Gem was wrapped around him, her lips on his skin nibbling and sucking as frantically as he felt.

"Don't care. Floor. Wall—"

"Wall?"

Oh, his sweet innocent. He latched onto her shirt and stripped the fabric off without bothering to unbutton it. "I'll show you sometime."

Not now. In fact, as much he wanted to simply throw her to the bed and thrust into her, he couldn't.

This lovemaking—with his mysterious memory gap—was their first time, and damn if he'd screw things up.

They got lost in the kissing business for a bit. Her mouth was warm and soft. Shaun held her, his thumb and fingers curled gently around the long column of her neck. Sweet. Intoxicating. It wasn't so much her flavour as the emotions that went along with the kiss. Knowing she was his, to care for, to be with.

Knowing she wanted him. Powerful, yet very intimidating.

Shaun leaned back to gaze into her eyes and fell headfirst.

119

What had he done to deserve her? Nothing. A big fat nothing. All his life he'd run from responsibility. From being the man he could have been. Maybe he'd done a few good things along the way, but that was in spite of himself, not because he planned it.

That was going to change, and now, because this woman before him, staring back at him?

She deserved more than he'd become.

But he'd work on the other parts of that later. Right now he was going to make love to his mate, and remember every single second. In minute detail.

Shaun stepped around her slowly, savouring the ability to run his hands over her body. The soft caress of her dark skin. The way his hand contrasted with hers. But more than the difference in their colouring, it was the ripple of goose bumps that rose behind his touch that drew his attention.

"Cold?" he pressed his lips against her upper arm.

"Hot. Crazy hot. Like I'm on fire and you're pouring on gasoline—oh..."

He licked her. A small, intimate touch as he held her in place. Another lick, this time lower. On the back of her arm. The next higher, at the ticklish spot where her arm met her body.

He tugged her bra strap to the side, letting the elastic fall away. More kisses followed, his actions repeated on the other side. Then he nuzzled her neck as he undid her bra and removed it completely.

She shivered.

Shaun pressed his naked chest to her back, the heat from both their bodies burning hotter than a blowtorch. Over her shoulder he admired her, the firm swells of her breasts, the slender curve of her waist. He teased her skin with tiny circles, starting at her hipbones, drawing his hands higher and higher. Dusting along her ribcage, skimming the underside of her breasts, caressing her collarbone.

Not one part of her upper body was neglected. Not one part was ignored, but nowhere received more than a brief caress before he moved on.

He was memorizing her. He'd forgotten their first lovemaking? This time would be etched into his memory forever.

Gem moaned as he cupped her breasts. "Feels so good."

"More?"

She nodded, leaning her weight on him. Her ass brushed his jeans, and the tight control he'd maintained nearly snapped. He ached.

Licking her nape was the only thing that calmed his wolf enough he could get the snap on her pants undone. "I like these, by the way."

She laughed. "Wearing pants feels as if I'm in a disguise."

He eased the zipper down, peeled the material off her hips. "No disguise, just being smart. These are what you'll need in the backcountry."

"So I'm not insane?"

"Right." He froze, only relaxing when she wiggled with laughter.

"Sorry, couldn't resist."

Neither could he. Shaun dropped to his knees behind her and nipped her butt cheek.

"Oh, what—?"

"Love the pants, love what's in them even more."

She smiled at him, and he was ready to do anything for her.

It took a long, long time to strip her. Every article of clothing he removed required him to lick and taste all the new exposed skin. By the time she was completely naked, he'd brought her close to orgasm with his fingers, his tongue, always stopping just before she gained release.

When he picked her up and laid her on the bed, her wolf was rumbling in pleasure.

Shaun paused to strip the rest of his clothing off, then crawled next to her, careful to push her hair aside. He looked her in the eye and let his fingers drop to her sex. Felt the wetness there. Used it to rub and caress until she shook. All the while he watched her. Saw her pupils change, her breathing hitch. She closed her eyes and her sheath squeezed around him, and he smiled.

It was only the beginning.

This time as he stroked, her breasts received attention. Laving and circling the tight peaks with his tongue, he waited until there was the tiniest of fluttering around his fingers, buried deep inside her. That's when he drew the entire tip into his mouth and sucked.

Gem screamed out in pleasure, thrashing on the bed as he refused to stop, pulling her up again and again until she quivered under his hands.

He finally covered her with his body. Nestled between her thighs. Rocked his hips a few times and enjoyed the way her cream coated him. Then he slipped the head of his cock into her heat, and they connected.

Wonderful, welcoming. Shaun fought to keep every memory fresh and new, but mostly what his brain told him was *holy fuck this feels incredible*. His mate fit him like no wolf ever had before. Like no one would in the future.

He rose on extended arms, and the only point they

physically connected was at the hips. He wanted more, wanted it all.

Gem drew up one leg and he slid a little deeper. "Sweet mercy."

"Shaun? You okay?"

Did he have to answer that? "I'm so okay, you can't imagine."

She shifted position again, and did this squeezy thing that made his eyes cross with pleasure. "Good. Then, can you move? Maybe?"

Shaun laughed. "Move how? Like this?"

A slow withdrawal was followed by an equally deliberate press forward. Every inch of her was incredible, wonderful and addictive.

"I like that." Gem arched her back as he brought their hips together, making the contact a little tighter, a little more intense.

He was going to lose his ever-loving mind at this rate.

A dozen measured strokes later he was praying for a miracle. If he didn't do something now—stop, recite the times table—*something*, he was about to go up in smoke.

Gem wrapped her legs around him and pulled violently, increasing his pace, and he was lost. They were making a memory, but now it was a heated and sweaty one, full of off-the-wall and borderline out-of-control energy.

When she cried out he nearly collapsed with happiness, not only because it was his name she called, but because he could finally allow himself to cross the line. He made one final thrust, stopping buried in her body, then let go.

The waves went on forever. Just freaking forever. It was nearly painful how good he felt, and his mind went blank.

*Oh, damn it, no.* Gem. Her name was Gem. They were mates...

Shaun rolled them both, draping her limp body over his. Panic faded as the details of their lovemaking remained strong, in spite of the lack of brainpower he currently possessed.

The usual lassitude of postcoital pleasure pooled in his limbs, along with an intriguing something extra. Making love with his mate? Far bigger, brighter and more *everything* than the physical rush of previous encounters. He stroked her back and sighed happily.

# Chapter Nine

Three days later and the sighing wasn't so happy anymore.

Gem sipped her tea as they waited for the breakfast bill. "Will we be leaving today or not yet?"

He shook his head. "Reports are that the herd is moving, but there's no use in heading anywhere this early."

She glanced out the window, her slim fingers tapping for a moment against her cup. "Okay, not much we can do about that."

Shaun was about ready to scream in frustration. Three days of cooling their heels. He'd taken her on a bus tour. They'd gone through all the museums—twice. They'd done everything he could think of that didn't require her getting dirty, muddy or dusty. Life had alternated between incredible and stinky, based on whether he'd remembered to shut the hell up and let her have some control, or if he'd flipped back into his usual *do as he pleased* mode.

It was a lot more difficult than he had thought it would be, to make a radical change in his life and attitude. At times it seemed he had made progress. Others? He was scared there was no freaking way this relationship would work. It was like tossing his wolf into the kitchen and demanding the beast make a gourmet meal. The result wouldn't look pretty even if he tried his damnedest.

She slipped her hand into his and squeezed for a moment. "Do you mind if I go write a few emails? Check my notes. Things like that."

A reprieve from planning another non-action fun-filled day? Shaun snatched at the opportunity. "Want me to walk you upstairs?"

She laughed. "I don't think so. I know the way by now."

"I'll be up in a bit. Maybe we can hit the casino again. Or go for a run? There's that great trail I told you about that allows easy access to the wilderness. The local pack uses it all the time. No one thinks anything of wolves in the area."

They still hadn't let their wolves out to play. A tiny crease appeared between her eyes, and he wondered how long her upbringing would remain a barrier. Any time he mentioned shifting she stiffened up. "No, that's okay. I'll see you whenever, all right?"

Shaun watched her walk away, remembering only after she'd left he should have held her chair. Done the polite thing.

He had managed to go a whole thirty minutes without swearing this morning. Fucking insanity, this learning-to-be-a-gentleman shit. Gem hadn't complained, but he felt as if there was some judging happening. Not so much her evaluating him, but their surroundings, the rustic nature of the hotel, the food.

Yeah, maybe his behavior at times as well.

He leaned back and stared out the window at the people walking past. His lack of finesse was a point in the north's favour—he bet she could never see him fitting in with her fancy highfaluting circumstances.

She was so skittish. He was not looking forward to the discussion he needed to have regarding the fine details of how the trip was going to go once they left Dawson, because she seemed determined to carry this thing through to the end.

In the meantime, they had at least three or four days to burn before the shit hit the fan. What to do with the time? She'd seemed enthusiastic about going for a run—*not*. And he didn't want to simply have sex.

Wait.

Well, he *wanted* to have sex, but that couldn't be the only thing they had going for them. Mating was on all kinds of levels. They had to connect, and so far, the bedroom was the one place they were completely at ease.

A whisper of a previous conversation drifted through his mind. He'd spent so much of his life doing for himself. Or even the things he'd done for others had the ulterior motive of screwing someone—usually someone in authority. He was a rebel without a cause. Learning to be special to Gem—well, he'd basically had no practice being special to *anyone* up to now.

*Be a hero.*

Shaun snuck a suspicious peek over his shoulder. No one there.

*Do the right thing, just because.*

He looked to the left, quickly discarding the idea that anyone in the restaurant had spoken to him. That meant it was one of the little inside voices taunting him. Damn it. Those were tougher ones to ignore.

Who had told him that? Do something for someone who can't even thank you. Just because it's the right thing to do.

He paid, then wandered outside to take a deep breath of the crisp air. The crowds were far thicker than they should be. One fellow stormed past, his shoulder bumping Shaun a trifle too hard, and he staggered to catch his balance.

He grabbed the nearest vertical object, which turned out to be the arm of a shifter who glared at his hand without a word.

*Freaking oversensitive asshole.*

Shaun let go and stepped back with exaggerated care. No use in getting into a fight when it wasn't needed. That's when he noticed exactly how many of the bodies on the street were shifters. And not just any shifters, but all kinds of bears. Hell, there were even a few polar shifters, and those dudes only left their turf in Churchill and the Far North once in a blue moon.

Shaun found a bench and sat for while, counting, wondering. This was the weirdest thing. Bear Jamboree or what?

The bench creaked beside him, and he glanced over, waving a finger when he recognized one of the local wolf pack.

"Nick."

"Shaun." Nick stretched his legs out in front of him as he surveyed the street, his easy positioning belying the tension in his body. "You come to watch the circus?"

Something *was* up. "I'm here with…a client."

It wasn't that he didn't want anyone else to know he and Gem were mates, but if there was trouble coming, he'd prefer to keep her out of it. He doubted rumbles were her forté.

Nick nodded. "Word is the bears are holding a rally—something about territorial divisions. A bear gathering is a rare enough occurrence, but with impeccable timing, the humans arranged a protest over the oil and gas development continuing up north. Two unpredictable groups in town at the same time? The sooner you can get out of Dodge the better your chances of avoiding any hassles."

Shaun twisted to face the older wolf. "Thanks for the warning. The pack got it under control?"

"We'll be fine." Nick ran a hand through his hair before gesturing to the street. "We get environmental protestors up here on a regular basis. They make some noise, wave a bunch of signs, then leave a mess behind on the streets. Pretty pathetic considering they shout 'save the earth' then litter like pigs."

A clatter rose to their right. Nick shot halfway out of his seat. Another man across the way waved him down, and Nick relaxed.

Impressive. "You got spotters coordinated?"

Nick nodded. "We know the signs, what to watch for, what to ignore. Right now, it's the humans getting riled up. All the bears who have arrived in the past couple days? They're behaving, but bears usually do. They like things orderly. Riots in the streets aren't their style, not unless they've been drinking."

The commotion quieted again. Shaun spoke before he could think it through. "Call me if you need help."

Nick eyed him with suspicion. "You looking for a new pack?"

*Shit.* "I'm not trying to take over or move up your ranks. Just a friendly offer is all."

Sheer disbelief painted Nick's expression. "Right."

*Fuck it.* Shaun rose and gave the other wolf a curt nod. He paced away, his mood increasingly foul.

How the hell could he convince Gem he was serious about being there for her when others pointed out so well he *didn't* know how to give unselfishly.

The boardwalk creaked under his feet, puffs of dust rising as he stomped his way down the street. Fine. Unselfish. What was the most unselfish thing he could think of to do?

Two complete revolutions of Main Street later he finally acknowledged the one obvious idea that wasn't totally crazy.

Find out what was up with the bears. Nick wasn't that high up the ranks in Dawson, so it was stupid expecting him to know if real trouble was brewing. Shaun needed to speak with the actual leaders, maybe offer Takhini's support—it couldn't hurt. He wondered momentarily if Evan would kick his ass for making the suggestion without checking in first.

Probably. *Shit.*

The memory of Gem's beautiful eyes staring at him with admiration... Shaun was ready to sell a bit of his soul to make her look at him like that all the time. It made his skin crawl, but he did it anyway. He hauled out his cell phone and called Evan.

"Moonshine Mayhem, director of Chaos speaking."

Shaun snorted. "Director, you got that right. Hey, why you being your own answering service? Where's Caroline?"

"Making a run down to the police station to bail out a few of the pack."

"No shit. Really? What they do?" Shaun paused to watch a taxi empty. Four bear shifters in fancy suits made their way up the stairs of the Grand Hotel, the valets rushing to bring in their cases.

"Got in a brawl down at the pizza parlour with a bunch of visiting bears. I let them cool their heels overnight before posting bail. Those boys are in for some hard labour when I get my hands on them." Evan spoke softly, but even Shaun heard the displeasure in his voice. Irreverent, yes, but his Alpha didn't tolerate the pack breaking his rules.

"Speaking of bears, that's why I'm calling. Dawson is overrun with them. You know anything about what's happening?"

Evan chuckled. "I know everything, man. It's politics. Every so many years—and no one seems to know exactly how many—

the bears meet to redistribute territory and such. Their hierarchy is way more formal than the way we wolves do things. They vote and shit."

No way. "Like, no beating each other up or ripping out throats for leadership? They vote on bits of paper and that decides the leaders?"

"Barbaric, isn't it?"

"Totally." They both laughed hysterically for a moment. Shaun took a deep breath. This stopping-being-Peter-Pan was tough. "Okay, level with me. If I suggested to the Dawson pack Takhini's got their back, would you agree or should I start running for Siberia?"

Dead silence greeted him. "Shaun, did I just hear you make a considered, grown-up suggestion all on your own?"

"Fuck you."

"Not really interested in swinging that way, darling. You should be getting enough from Gem—oh, wait a minute. That's what this is all about, isn't it? You trying to impress your new lady?"

His Alpha was far too close to the mark. Shaun resumed pacing the boardwalk. "I repeat, fuck you."

Evan laughed at him. "Aren't you supposed to be guiding your mate somewhere into the bush for the next couple weeks? Is this like last fall when you caused all kinds of mischief and then took off?"

Shaun growled. "Hardly. Last year I purposely hid so you couldn't order me to tell you where I'd taken my friends for a little private R&R. This go-round I have to leave, which is why I suggested Takhini as a backup, not just me."

"So last year you flaunted my authority, this time you're asking for permission?"

The answer stuck in his throat. "*Argh.* Um, maybe."

Evan crowed. "Sweet. You beg so well..." Shaun opened his mouth, "...and don't bother to tell me to fuck anything."

*Bastard.*

His Alpha continued, all humour and joking vanished. "Here's the deal. Tell them we're available if they need us. I've got three other outlying packs that owe me favours. If trouble arises, Dawson can call. Rumor is the first stages of the bears' meetings are in Dawson City. Second set might move our direction. I hope the northern packs will reciprocate if we need a hand."

Shaun nodded. "Makes sense. I'll drop in on them this morning."

"Last thing. This has to stay quiet. Remind Dawson of that as well. Keep an eye on what's happening with the bears, but any wolf alliances are to remain hush-hush. Bears are usually reasonable creatures, but if they think they're about to be overrun by pack, things could get out of hand."

That made sense. Shaun scratched his head. "How come I didn't know any of this? Did the meetings and shit just start in the last couple days?"

Again, silence for a moment. "Nah. There's been signs for a while. You've had things on your mind."

Shaun swore. That was bullshit, and they both knew it.

The light laughter on the other end of the line was both annoying and reassuring, it was so Evan. "Look. You have a good idea here. Roll with it. Forget the past and move forward. Oh, and have a great time with Gem, okay? Shit. Gotta run. The screw-ups are back, and I have to go put the fear of their Alpha into them. Call me if you need anything."

Shaun hung up, feeling slightly dirty. This following-the-rules thing wasn't...normal.

The scent of unwashed bodies struck him with the force of a brick wall. There were times having enhanced smelling ability sucked. The solid pack of people milling in front of the bar doors and blocking his path didn't budge as he shouldered through.

He sidestepped a familiar-looking dark-haired brute already teetering drunkenly at barely noon. It was the biggest of the bears Shaun had thrown out of the Moonshine Pub only a few days ago. Obviously even the lowest class of bear was involved in these talks.

Shaun glanced down the street and considered. If he was going to be all self-sacrificing and shit, he may as well start right now. Armed with Evan's permission—*gag*—Shaun turned toward the Dawson pack house.

One final concern hit as he marched toward his goal. Potential shifter wars were nothing he wanted Gem to worry about. As if crazed politics were a selling feature that would entice her to settle in the north. No, he'd have to find some way to do what he needed to without letting her know he was potentially knee deep in trouble. Situation normal, all fucked up.

She shouldn't be upset. He hadn't done anything wrong.

Had he?

Gem tried to remember the specific details of what they'd talked about right before she left the breakfast table.

Her stomach grumbled for the fifteenth time in the past half hour.

"Fudge."

She opened the curtain and stared into the street. It was nearly six. She hadn't gone downstairs to grab lunch, thinking Shaun would return at any minute. There had to be a mistake. He couldn't have meant to leave her alone all day. Or...had he said he'd see her at supper?

Her phone rang, and she stared at the display with rising frustration. Her father. Again.

She clicked off the ringer and threw the phone on the bed.

It bounced a foot.

The small act of violence was so satisfying, she moved without thinking. Picked up the phone, stepped back a couple additional paces. Cocked her arm and flung her cell harder than previously. It bounced higher.

Not enough. She grabbed it again, raced across the room, her back to the door and took a couple of running steps. This time when she let go, she spat out the word even louder.

"Fudge!"

The phone bounced, hit the edge of the lamp, ricocheted sideways and crashed into the garbage can. Both tipped in opposite directions, and she watched in horror as they landed, the can softly, the lamp with a terrifying crash.

"That was interesting."

Gem twirled, covering her heated cheeks as she stared into Shaun's laughing eyes.

"I, um..."

"Didn't like the décor?"

There really was something happening in this northern air. Her hands shook in aggravation as she moved to clean up the mess. "I'm sorry, I don't usually do things like that."

Shaun was at her side, grabbing the garbage can and holding it for her. "Hey, I don't mind. If I'm not on the receiving end of the throwing, it's kinda fun to watch."

She dropped another shard of pottery into the can. *Great.* Now she was back to entertaining people. Gem clamped her teeth together and concentrated on moving the lampshade from where it lay tangled around the side table.

He caught her wrist and held her immobile. "Hey."

Gem sighed as she examined his face.

There was no longer amusement there. "I wasn't trying to insult you. I think what I said came out wrong. You okay? Why are you throwing things in the first place?"

An ache pulsed inside. "My father."

Shaun lifted her off her knees and took her to the couch. "I thought you got along with your old man."

"I do, except for him forgetting that I'm not a baby, and that I'd like to have some control over my own life."

Shaun leaned back, keeping her hands in his. "Did you call him?"

She shook her head. Layers of guilt, deep and colourful, had made her almost break her promise to herself and contact him. "He doesn't know."

Shaun frowned. "Know what?"

"About us."

Shaun sucked in air. "Oh damn, I was going to ask you about that. I mean, I bet you've got all kinds of traditional shit that...I mean protocol that I should be doing. Like calling him and telling him we are mates and—"

"I don't want to." She couldn't read his reaction. Was that panic or relief? "I mean, I want him to know, and he's a great dad and all, but he's used to getting his way, and until we figure this out..." She waved a hand between them. Oh dear, what a mess she was.

Shaun caressed her fingers. "I think I know what you mean, but I'm serious. If there's something I can do to help, tell me?"

She nodded. "I will."

They sat quietly for a minute, then he leaned forward, curiosity on his face.

"So, why the baseball with the phone?"

She pointed to the desk where she'd spread out her work. "I've been going through my notes. The information I need to gather to complete my report. And suddenly it all seemed stupid. A total waste of time and money. I'm a small cog in a tiny wheel. What difference does it make if I do this or not?"

"Hell. Your research makes a huge difference."

That was not what she'd expected to hear. "Really?"

Shaun's mouth twisted into a wry grin. "Okay, earlier I said you were insane—I mean, we thought the scientist who booked the trip was insane. And we do need to talk about the details, but the actual reason you're here isn't the study, right? I mean, really, *really* why you're here."

Gem collapsed back against the couch to stare across at him. Her studies had originated from her interest in science and the environment, that was true. But arranging a project that required a trip that would take her as far away from home possible?

That had nothing to do with scientific discovery, and everything to do with discovering herself.

"I just want to prove I can make it on my own. For a little while."

Shaun snorted. "And then I drop into your life, and you're still not alone. Not even after traveling all that distance." He lifted her knuckles and kissed them lightly. "I'm sorry for crowding you, but I'm not sorry I found you."

Gem couldn't talk for a moment, her throat was so tight. She nodded. "Me too. I'm just so all over the place right now—both my mind and my emotions. What if all this time they've all been humouring me? My professor, my fellow students? Maybe I *don't* belong anywhere but protected and under the firm control of—"

"Bullshit." Shaun leapt to his feet and towered over her. "Where the hell did that come from? Where's the woman who less than a week ago told me and my wolf to cool our jets?"

She stared in shock. "I didn't say that to you."

He laughed. "No, you told me it was 'more appropriate to continue with my usual systematic preparations and consider our attachment to be on a temporary hiatus'."

Gem cradled her head in her hands. "I can't believe I said that when I really didn't want to send you away. I also don't want to make my father unhappy, but him calling me all the time, and emailing—I wish he wouldn't, and yet I miss him terribly. It's so confusing."

A pair of dusty shoes moved into her line of vision as he squatted in front of her. "I'm with you on that one, love. I've never been so wishy-washy before in my fucking, I mean, my entire life."

They stared at each other, and a tiny strand of electricity slid from where his hands rested on her knees. The sensation wasn't sexual, not this time. It was cool and calming. Like a hands-on application of peace, and Gem leaned her head against his shoulder.

They sat like that for a while, breathing slowly. Drawing strength from each other. Finally, he wrapped an arm around her and changed position to sit at her side. They leaned back, her head on his chest, his hands stroking her hair, her cheek.

Her neck.

"Surprise, surprise—there are layers to this mate thing." Shaun spoke quietly.

Gem had never experienced anything like it before. "I don't feel so worried anymore."

"It's the connection between us. Being mates will help us through all kinds of situations. I've heard others talk about it, but man—that was cool. Totally new."

Mates had many deep levels of connection, and in the midst of her other concerns, she'd completely forgotten something. "Shaun, can you hear me talk to you?"

His soft laugh stroked her. "Umm, yeah?"

"No, not this way." She sat up and turned to face him. "In your head."

"Hell. I haven't." Shaun stopped and stared at her, obviously attempting to say something. She waited.

He waited.

Nothing happened.

Shaun grunted in frustration. "It's not working. Maybe we won't have a mate connection like that. It's one of those things, some do, some don't. Or we need more practice."

That didn't make sense. "But when we made love the first time, I heard you."

"Really?"

"I told you, remember?"

His mouth opened, then closed and his gaze darted away. "Umm, no. Forgot...about that."

Sadness hit again, the tranquility of the previous moments diluted by a sense of loss. "Do you ever think we'll be able to?"

There was a trace of something—worry? fear?—on his face,

right before he smiled and tweaked her nose. "We might need to exercise more or something. Remember, we only met a few days ago. And we haven't had the chance to do a lot of things, not even go for a run together. Let's give it time."

She still felt as if there was something he wasn't telling her, but after the closeness they'd shared, she didn't want to damage their fragile intimacy.

The rumbling in her stomach provided as good a topic change as anything.

He pulled her to her feet. "Sounds as if we need supper, then we have to pack. I suggest we head out tomorrow."

Gem moved toward her suitcase. "Really? The herd is that close?"

"No, but remember I mentioned Chicken? We're going to wait there for a bit. It should be a little quieter than here and more things to look around at. We've kind of done Dawson to death."

He made himself busy. Gem watched in confusion as he untied and tied his laces. Twice. What was going on?

"Shaun?"

He snapped his head up. "Yup? Ready to go?"

She hurried to finish changing. "In a minute. By the way, where were you today? I thought we were going to go do something. When you didn't come back, I was worried."

Pacing. He was definitely pacing. "Sorry about that. Just got caught up talking with people. That's all."

Suspicion grew. "What people?"

"People." He glanced at his watch. "Oh my, look at time. If we want to find a seat we'd better—"

"Shaun, where were you?"

He reached for her hand, and she reluctantly allowed him

to take it. "I was talking to some of the locals, and I lost track of the time. Sorry."

His dark eyes shone with sincerity. Then he switched topics, becoming utterly charming and entertaining for the rest of the evening. As much as she'd loved the closeness they had shared, there was something marring the joy of it.

She still wanted to know where he'd gone.

# Chapter Ten

The expression of delight on Gem's face was so endearing Shaun found himself tripping as he walked down the street by her side, attempting to catch every nuance. The town of Chicken was pretty cool. It had changed in the past couple of years, becoming more of a touristy getaway spot for shifters, and less one-hole-away-from-the-entrance-to-nowhere.

There was none of the gold-rush paraphernalia that was featured so prominently in Whitehorse and Dawson. Town council and the planning board weren't trying to impress visitors with historical tidbits. With the number of packs, prides and clans that made their home in the area, the goal was to maintain positive relations among the various factions. That resulted in a multitude of coffee shops, boutiques and half a dozen bakeries all piping glorious scents onto Main Street.

Shifters liked their goodies.

When a wolverine in furry form dashed past them, shifted to human and calmly walked naked into the nearest store, Gem's little gasp made him chuckle.

"What?"

Gem pointed, then dropped her hand and tangled her fingers together. "Right out in public? What if someone had seen her? I mean, someone human?"

Shaun gestured the length of the street. "Look around.

Chicken is on the Top of the World Highway, and the shortest distance from outside civilization to here is a four-hour drive in either direction. The few humans who do make the trip slip right on through. They never stay in town long. We talked about it once, a group of friends and me. The nearest thing we could figure is that with how many shifters live here there's something in the air that makes humans uncomfortable, so they just keep on driving."

She shook her head. "Everywhere we go you manage to find new things to surprise me. It's—"

Caught in mid-pivot, her words froze on her tongue. He rotated to see what she'd discovered to make her expression change that much, that fast. R-rated movie theater? Adult toy store?

A couple stood a few feet from them, kissing. Shaun hesitated. Didn't seem too risqué to him, but who knows what was the norm for her back home.

"Do you see that?" He could barely hear her, the words whispered so soft and low.

He squeezed her fingers. "I...ah, yeah."

The couple pressed tighter together, the woman getting into it, her hands buried in the guy's hair. The man grabbed her ass, and even as Shaun watched, lifted one of her legs to wrap the limb around his hip. Shaun sighed happily. Shifters were so cool about sex.

"I wonder if it would be comfortable?" Gem leaned into his side.

Comfortable? His cock wasn't comfortable. The damn thing had risen and now pushed urgently against the front of his jeans. "Oh, I think it would be just dandy."

Gem's eyelashes fluttered, and she stared at him sweetly. "Do you think that would look good on me?"

Draped over his body, lips locked together and one second away from being screwed in the street? *Hell, yeah.* "I think you were made for it."

He reached for her, biting back a curse as she slipped out of reach. Gem dodged the groping couple and ran toward a nearby shop.

Shaun stood in one spot, frozen in confusion.

"Shaun. You coming?"

*No.* It seemed not. At least not the way he wanted to be. What was going on? He shook his head and concentrated harder on her than the ache in his groin. She had the door to the shop open and hovered in the doorway.

Nope, still clueless. He glanced at the couple again in envy. They had taken all of four steps farther down the street to finish pressed against the side of the building, frantically stripping each other. The shop door shut, and Gem's figure appeared in the feature glass as she pointed between two dresses displayed on mannequins.

Oh shit. She was talking about shopping, not very Public Displays of Affection.

Okay, he could do shopping. If he had to. He followed her slowly and made plans for at least ravishing her in his mind as he watched her try on outfits.

A guy had to have a little fun.

Gem glided through the restaurant door ahead of Shaun, the loose edge of her new dress skimming her thighs. Her skin tingled as if touched with tiny sparks. The delight racing through her wasn't just from the nearly scandalous length of the cut. It wasn't the material itself, with the softness of silk and the teeniest touch of lace stroking her like a million tiny butterfly wings.

It was the way Shaun couldn't stop staring at her that made the dress worthwhile.

He slipped a hand around her waist and led her to their table, the heat of his touch bleeding through the light layer separating them. Everything was perfect, the way they brushed together intimately as he seated her, the way his gaze kept roaming over her body as they ordered, sipped drinks, ate.

She could barely swallow, her throat tightening as the sexual tension intensified. Whatever lingering annoyances she'd experienced during the tail end of their time in Dawson were washed away by his current attentiveness.

When she stood to take a bathroom break, he leapt to his feet, helping with her chair and stroking his fingers over her shoulders as she left.

Her entire stroll toward the back of the room she swore his gaze never moved off her hips.

An assortment of emotions danced through her as she primped in front of the mirror. Having found her mate was beginning to feel more—right. More like something she could balance in her life, and less like another older male ordering her around. Oh, she was unsure how she was going to convince him to move south, but that wasn't as important right now as making sure they were okay as a couple. And while sex wasn't the only thing they should base their relationship on, it wasn't a bad place to start.

She smoothed her hands down the front of her dress, enjoying the soft caress over her bare legs. Against the nearly naked skin of her lower body. Shaun had no idea she'd found a pair of very sexy underwear to accompany her dress. She wondered what he would do when he made the discovery?

Something wonderfully wicked and intensely pleasurable, that was for sure. Yeah, the *starting with sex* part was working out fine.

While the future stretched out unknown, there was no doubt in her mind what the rest of today would look like. She was going to go back into the restaurant and knock his socks off, figuratively. Then, after they'd finished dinner and maybe danced a little, it was back to the hotel where she would literally take care of incidentals like socks, shoes and everything else he wore.

Of course, returning to their table and finding it empty put a crimp in her plans.

His jacket lay draped over the armrest, but there was no sign of him anywhere. She stood, hands resting on the back of her chair, slightly disoriented.

*Get a grip, girl.*

He must have gone to the washroom. Gem sat, feeling foolish she'd hesitated for even a minute. She sipped her water and examined the décor.

Then she heard his laugh, and it hadn't come from anywhere in the dining room. Gem rose and slipped through the doorway separating the restaurant from the bar. She leaned against the nearest wall, waiting for her eyes to adjust to the lower lighting.

It only took a second to spot him standing next to an extremely pretty woman. The petite lynx shifter was perched on a barstool, her silver-blonde hair tossed over one shoulder in gorgeous smooth sweeps. Gem touched her own head, smoothing down the usual errant strands with fingers suddenly gone numb.

The woman reached out and planted a hand against Shaun's chest, and Gem's temper flared.

That was *her* mate. Gem straightened, intending to go and rip the woman's head off, or some equally undignified thing, when a touch landed on her shoulder. She turned to look into the buttons lining the shirt of the largest man she'd ever seen. Tilted her head up. Up. Way up.

Dark crew cut. Sparkling green eyes. Broad didn't even start to describe his shoulders. He had a different scent to him—bear shifter all the way, but not one she was familiar with. A cocky smile played around his mouth, and he tipped his head politely. "Hey. You wanna dance?"

An instant rejection shot to her lips, trapped when a repeat of Shaun's laughter carried over and sealed her mouth shut. Pain rippled through her, and she fought the violent urge to be ill. No, no cowering in the corner allowed—this was a far better idea. She would see what Shaun thought of *her* stepping out on him. If moving from woman to woman was what being mated meant here in the north, she wanted to know right now.

Handing him a little of his own medicine felt more than justified.

Gem put aside every instinct in her that screamed *noooo* and smiled sweetly at the giant. "I would love to."

She placed her fingers in his and allowed him to guide her onto the crowded floor.

He was a decent enough lead, which let her totally ignore her footing. While she usually loved to dance, this time she was more interested in darting glances between the other bodies weaving around them. Not that she wanted to see Shaun's reaction when he realized someone was paying attention to her. No, she was totally uninterested.

The stranger placed a hand on her lower back and tugged her closer. Gem took a quick internal inventory, hoping to find a flicker of interest, some kind of sexual response to being in another man's arms. Nothing. It was like dancing with her grampa.

The big shifter was a good-looking fellow, but now that she'd met her mate, it was clear there was a downside to not being with Shaun. She simply didn't want this man touching her. How could Shaun even think of being with another woman? It made no sense. Her partner guided her to the side to avoid a drunkard teetering past them.

"Sorry about that." Her dance partner leaned down to speak into her ear. "That guy's not from here. Not sure what he's doing."

It seemed obvious to Gem. Falling down in the middle of the dance floor. Even the protective arm around her wasn't enough to allow the butterflies of fear to settle as the noise level increased, loud shouts and insults traded between the drunk and another couple men at the bar. She peeked in Shaun's direction again, hating that it was his embrace she wanted to be sheltered in.

Across the room, for a split second, they made eye contact. Shaun's expression passed instantly from shock into sheer rage before disappearing behind the rising head of the drunken bear as he attempted to regain his feet.

"Hey, pretty lady. I like you."

A big hand pawed the front of her dress before she could step back, her companion forcing an opening in the crowds to let them escape.

"Get your hands off my mate." Shaun's voice echoed off the roof, cutting through the dance music pounding the room.

Oh, *now* she was his mate? Gem sniffed and moved a step closer to her dance partner.

It was right about then that all hell broke lose.

Shaun stepped onto a bar stool and leapt into the air. The drunken bear made it to his feet just in time to become a landing pad for Shaun's descending body, and they both tumbled back to the floor. A loud grunt of pain escaped the bear, screams rang in the background and Gem was pushed to her knees as a chair flew overhead.

"Crawl toward the exit," her partner ordered, covering her with his body as bottles and plates crashed around them.

"Gem!"

She peeked out from under her protective block to see Shaun scrambling upright, only to have a hand snag his ankle and yank him off balance. He kicked backward, connecting a foot with the bear's face. A roar of anger was followed by a violent swing of arms, and Shaun went down in a tangled mess with the flailing bear.

She was tugged away from the center of the room as the giant bear attempted to get her to safety. Leaving Shaun behind—it was so wrong. Everything in her wanted to stay back and help him. Anger rose—why couldn't she just turn and walk away? Why should she feel anxious for him when he'd been cheating on her, talking to another woman?

*Because talking is one step away from sex, right?*

Oh...pickles.

Maybe she'd misunderstood the situation. Even as guilt struck, a loud screeching sound rang from the left, and she glanced over to see a tall buffet descending toward her. There was no time to retreat, too many bodies between her and escape. She threw up her arms and hoped for the best.

Something hard and warm crashed into her, pulling her to the ground and rolling them both to safety under the feet of the roaming crowds.

"Hold on to me," Shaun shouted above the noise, and

Gem's heart pounded as she obeyed. She snapped one arm around his neck, clinging tight as he cradled her to his body and plunged them forward through the masses toward where the cooler night air poured in the open front door.

She cried as a blow landed on her side. Shaun rolled them again, blocking her from the attack even as he managed to get them free from the mess and out into the relative calm of the street.

There were shifters everywhere, in human and animal form. The fights continued, but the scene around them blurred as Gem clutched Shaun with a death grip and allowed him to sweep her up in his arms to carry her away.

"Are you okay?" He paused outside a shop to run a quick gaze over her. "Damn it, Gem, when I saw you go down, I thought I would die."

Her side ached, but the look in his eyes made things infinitely better. Then she noticed he was bleeding.

"I'm okay, but your face—"

He'd been hit, a ribbon of blood trickling from the cut on his forehead. "Those damn bears. I'll be fine, but they are acting awfully weird—even for grizzlies."

"You bastard. Ready to take your medicine?"

Raucous shouts rose from the street behind them, and Gem cowered against Shaun's side as he cradled her protectively. A crowd of dark bodies had surrounded one figure—the man she'd been dancing with. Two of the group smacked him on the back and sent him sprawling to his knees. He rolled, but couldn't escape before another shifter landed on top of him and began to systematically pound blows against his unprotected face.

Gem's throat tightened. She had no idea what was going on, but didn't think anyone deserved this kind of abuse. She

149

tugged on Shaun's arm.

"He's all by himself, seven against one? What could he have done? I didn't see him do anything wrong."

Shaun nodded once. "Even if he did, this isn't the way to deal with it."

He squeezed her tight before turning toward the street.

Gem stepped after him. "Should I...?"

He twirled to face her. "You stay out of it, okay?"

"But I can—"

"Stay out of it." He clamped onto her arms and stared her in the eye. "I can't fight if I'm worried about you. Please."

It only took a second for her to nod, and when he pointed to a nearby doorway, she fled in obedience. It didn't matter how strong she was as a wolf, not when other kinds of shifters were involved.

From the safety of the entranceway, she turned to watch as he waded back into the fray. Fists flying, feet kicking. The match was hard and dirty, but Shaun moved with an easy grace, mowing down bodies in his path one by one until he reached the centre of the fight and peeled the two main opponents apart.

"Is he your mate?" a feminine voice asked from beside her.

Gem refused to look away, cringing as a blow rocked Shaun. "Yes. What's happening?"

"The bears have some kind of territorial battle brooding. There is supposed to be a peaceful gathering in Dawson, but a few side agendas seem to be heating up their blood. Martin—the one getting the shit kicked out of him—he's local. I'm surprised he's involved, he's not usually into politics."

"Is there someone who can stop this?" Martin was back on his feet, standing shoulder to shoulder with Shaun as the

150

circling group of bears took random swings and lunges their direction.

"Like the police?"

"Yes." Gem slammed a hand over her mouth to capture her gasp of fear. Shaun ducked at the last moment before landing a solid punch on another attacker.

"There are times it's better to let the guys beat each other senseless. Being shifters and all, it gets messy when they think they're being bossed around, especially by us females."

Gem snuck a quick peek to her side and finally saw who stood next to her. "Oh. It's you."

The lynx shifter who had been with Shaun in the bar eyed her curiously. "You have an issue with me, sweetie?"

The intensity of Gem's simmering fear as it burst into blazing anger surprised her. "Hands off my mate from now on, okay?"

The woman backed up. "Hey, I'm all about the peaceful stuff. No problem."

Someone called out *Nadia*, and the lynx turned, waving her hand at the summons as if annoyed. Gem spotted an abandoned walking stick leaning against the wall beside the door, and desperation sent a terrible idea into her head.

She snatched up the stick. Her mate was in trouble, and she was not going to stand there and watch.

"What are you doing?" Nadia asked.

*Besides shaking with fear?* "Letting them fight is not the way to solve matters. Fighting is childish and unproductive."

Gem slipped toward the street. In the short time she'd had her attention elsewhere, Shaun and Martin had knocked another couple of the gang to the ground, but there was blood pouring down Martin's arm, and more smeared across Shaun's face. Gem swallowed hard. Getting involved wasn't what Shaun had asked for, but she simply couldn't stand there and watch him be outnumbered.

She raced forward and swung with all her might.

Of course, if she hadn't squeezed her eyes shut, she would have had a better chance of hitting any one. The sudden *thunk* as the stick made contact with something surprised her enough her eyes popped open just in time to see one of the bears go down with a satisfying crash.

That's when she realized she was a touch too close to the continuing action, and twirled to race out of reach.

A cooling mist floated past her.

Gem stared at the sky in confusion, looking for a cloud, or barring that, a water hose being used on the fighters, but there was nothing. Still, her heart rate slowed, and the stick grew impossibly heavy. The impromptu weapon slipped from her fingers as the blonde lynx walked past.

Nadia stepped over the prone bodies to stare in disgust. "What a waste of energy, boys. You want to fight, do it properly. Give us time to organize bets and make it a real evening's entertainment. Otherwise, you simply piss off the locals, and that's no fun for anyone."

One of the men snarled at her, and she planted her fists on her hips and glared harder.

He dropped to his knees without another sound.

"See, that's what I mean. When you're all growly and stuff? No one likes you." She clapped her hands and motioned to the bar with her head. "Everyone, time to cool down. Grab a broom, get that dance floor cleaned up and go back to relaxing. No more fights tonight. Got it?"

A steady stream of curse words spilled from the lips of one

of the fallen bears. Shaun pointed toward him. "You have a first aid center in town? That one needs more than a beer."

Nadia motioned at the crowd, and a couple stepped forward to pull the bear away, his heels dragging on the ground. All the tension in the air simply dissipated, and understanding finally hit Gem. She turned to stare at the lynx in wonder.

"You're an Omega—and you can control all the shifters." Gem had never heard of pack hierarchy crossing shifter species boundaries before.

The blonde blinked at her. "And you're black."

Gem paused, taken aback for a moment. "What's that—?"

"Getting described like that is rather offensive, isn't it? Because that's not all you are. Don't define me by the obvious."

Shaun had a supporting arm around Martin, and a disapproving frown on his face as they paced forward. "Cut her some slack, Nadia. She didn't mean anything by it."

A smile twisted the corner of Nadia's mouth. "So the mighty Shaun is mated. I'm interested to hear how this turns out."

"You know each other?" Gem eyed them suspiciously.

The blonde batted her eyelashes. "No worries, it was a long time ago. He's all yours now. Really, I don't poach."

Gem jerked back, moving toward her mate instinctively.

Martin pushed off Shaun's assistance. "Thanks for calming things down."

"Part of the job, you know." The blonde held up her hands like they were guns, blew smoke from the tips and pretended to holster them.

"Sheriff Nadia. Good one."

She turned and walked away.

Martin sighed, then faced Shaun. Gem slipped in close,

tucking herself against his torso. Her pounding heart matched the tempo of his.

The bear shifter held out his hand and Shaun shook it. "Thank you. There's bad blood between that clan and mine. I appreciated your help."

"No worries. Shit this bad happen around here often?"

The big shifter laughed, the sound turning into a groan as he wrapped an arm around his ribs. "The fights? Off and on all winter. Typical shifter stuff. But with territorial debates going on, tempers amongst the bears are running shorter than usual. The ballots close in a month or so. Until then, there's a lot of maneuvering happening. Plus, the more unscrupulous clans are going after the undecided with intimidation, or buying their votes outright."

"I'll say it again, you bears have weird ways." Shaun squeezed her shoulders, his touch reassuring. Most of the discussion washed over Gem. All she wanted to do was to haul Shaun aside and make sure he was okay.

It seemed to take forever to get back to their hotel room after they said their farewells to Martin, the big man rumbling down the street, small clusters of shifters moving away as he passed.

Gem stared into the mirror at Shaun as he removed his shirt. He groaned as the material slipped from his shoulders. She helped him tug the fabric free, noting the bruises rising on his torso.

"You're a mess." She pressed a kiss to his chest as a penance for her words.

He cupped her face, letting his gaze trickle down her body. Her new dress was dirty and ripped, the pretty fabric stained from a combination of liquids off the barroom floor and the dust of the street.

The expression in his eyes—she'd never felt more beautiful.

"I should be a mess. That was a hell of a lot of bears." He leaned closer and touched his lips to hers before groaning again.

She rushed to turn on the shower and help finish stripping his clothes off. "You were very brave."

"I was?" He shuddered as the water landed. Gem tore off her tattered dress and grabbed a facecloth, stepping into the shower with him. His eyes were closed, but he smiled as she touched the soaking cloth to his torso to clean away the blood and dust from the fight.

"You were. I was proud of you."

"You were mad at me."

Well, yes, that too. "Shaun, what were you doing with Nadia?"

He sighed, a weary sound full of confusion. "Same thing I was doing back in Dawson when you got mad at me for not explaining myself. I was looking for information, trying to make sure... Well, it's northern politics and I didn't think you'd be interested."

She stroked the cloth over his right pectoral and higher to where his shoulder muscle bulged. With every touch he responded, a small moan or a twitch. Gem wiggled behind him and carried on, thinking hard. He had known she was upset in Dawson and didn't say anything.

Was it really something she needed to get all the details about right now?

The steam built around them, thickening the air on every breath she took, and clouding the sight of his smooth flesh only inches away from her. Slicking her fingers over his skin made the connection between them burst upward, a longing for his touch overwhelming the need for answers.

Gem leaned her cheek against him, her hands resting on his hips. He threaded his fingers through hers, his thumbs rubbing gently back and forth.

One small lean brought their bodies into full contact, her breasts pressed to his back.

"Gem..."

She shushed him, gyrating an inch at a time, letting the moisture of the shower become the only barrier between their flesh. Shaun tilted his face upward and let the spray hit him fully in the face.

Gem snuck her palm forward, leaving his hip. His hand stayed behind for a moment, his fingers stroking her forearm, tightening into a firm clasp as she made contact with his groin. She continued until his erection filled her hand, the hot, heavy length pulsing as she closed her fingers and stroked.

The splash of the water against the tiles faded into the background as his moans filled her ears.

"Gem..."

The timbre of agony mixed with ecstasy in his voice made her smile. "Like this?"

He nodded, his hand covering hers and tightening. Increasing the length of her stroke, then shortening it. His fingers urged her on, forceful, then relaxing away as he rocked his hips, thrusting into her hand.

There were too many sensations to keep track of them all. Touching him made her achy inside, and the noises from his lips made her even hotter. Knowing she brought him pleasure after the pain he'd received—giving to him filled an enormous need.

This was another part of being mates. She took a deep

breath through her nose, thrilling at the mixture of their scents. He squeezed her left hand where it rested on his hip, pressing harder into her right hand. He shuddered, and his shaft jerked, the heat of his seed splashing her fingers.

Shaun turned and half-collapsed against the shower wall, his head resting on the tiles as he pulled her into his arms. "When my brain comes back online I plan on making your world spin at least as hard as you just—holy fucking hell."

He gasped for air, and Gem bit back the giggles. His swearing didn't upset her this time. Neither did the fact he'd kept a secret from her. In fact, she was sure right now there wasn't much that could upset her.

When he kissed her, his hands pulling back her hair and beginning a slow seduction of all her senses, she felt as if life was pretty much as perfect as it could get.

Then he slipped to his knees, and the moment got even better. Gem closed her eyes and let her mate love her.

# Part Three

I wanted the gold, and I sought it,
I scrabbled and mucked like a slave.
Was it famine or scurvy—I fought it;
I hurled my youth into a grave.
I wanted the gold, and I got it—
Came out with a fortune last fall,—
Yet somehow life's not what I thought it,
And somehow the gold isn't all.

*"The Spell of the Yukon"—Robert Service*

# Chapter Eleven

There were aches on his pains when Shaun woke, but the physical ailments weren't the first things to catch his attention.

Nope, it was the way Gem was all snuggled up tight against him, her cheek resting on his chest. One hand wrapped around his biceps as if she was never letting him go. The list of shit to figure out remained huge, but the list of things he liked about the mating deal grew bigger all the time.

He kissed the top of her head and eased himself away. She wiggled and sighed drowsily, burrowing back into the blankets. He didn't have the heart to wake her since this would be her last day in civilization for a while. She refused to abandon her research project.

No matter how much he'd come to admire her, ensuring she knew the realities involved in their upcoming trip was going to be nasty.

Shaun stretched one arm, then the other, pleased with the result. The damage was minor relative to how he could have felt. He had been beat up, torn up and kicked around a lot worse before. If he had taken the time last night to change into his wolf and back he would have been less stiff this morning, but Gem hadn't wanted to shift, and she'd been far too enticing in her human form to leave for long.

The sex had done wonders for making him feel better.

Add in the fact the pains were from performing a totally unselfish act of kindness—he was still grinning when he caught a glimpse of himself in the mirror. He'd done something because it was the right thing to do. Not to screw anyone, or get screwed, even though that had been a bonus side effect. Yup, the fight had been pretty damn cool.

There was just one cloud hanging over his head. Somehow in the next couple days, he needed to decide both the best time and the best way to double-check that Gem understood the road was about to get a lot rougher.

He chose wrong.

"What do you mean 'if I want to cancel the trip'?"

Shaun cringed, glancing around the hangar to see if anyone else had heard the outburst. So she did have a volume other than soft and gentle. "Gem, we can't disturb the caribou. There's a minimum fly-by radius we aren't allowed to break— the cows are more susceptible to loud noises when they're pregnant, so the government increased the permissible space between any public disturbances and the animals."

Gem stepped back, crossed her arms and glared at him. "I'm not an idiot. I'm well aware of the rules regarding the herd. Research paper, remember?"

"Right. Then you know that while we can approach the birthing grounds ahead of time to get your information, we need to retreat to a protected location to make further observations. We can't take the chopper. We have to land and hike in."

Her eyes narrowed to evil slits. "Are you deliberately trying to be offensive, or is this just coming naturally to you?"

Shaun studied the ceiling in the hope inspiration would strike. He thought through all his words, attempting to figure out what he'd done to piss her off this thoroughly.

162

Nope. Nada.

"I can honestly say I don't have a freaking clue what you're so upset about."

Gem gave her head a violent shake. "You basically told me that after being in the north for nearly two weeks, you don't want me to complete the research I came to do. At least, that's what I heard."

"Wait, no, I just wanted to be positive you know the specifics. This isn't going to be a one-day stroll in the park."

"Shaun, I'm well aware the only way in and out of the area is on foot. Why do you think I brought hiking boots? Why I've been training for the distances we'll need to travel?"

*She had?* "Really?"

"Why is that so impossible to believe?" Gem crossed her arms and glared at him. "Just because I don't cuss and slouch all over the place doesn't mean I'm not an intelligent, capable woman."

"I never said you—"

"Asking me if I want to bow out at this point is like saying it."

"But I—"

"And assuming because I have soft hands that automatically means I'm a spoiled, lazy creature is insanity on your part, not mine."

"Right, and I'm sorry—"

"Plus, you did agree to guide me. If you had an issue there should have been a formal complaint made way back even before I arrived."

"Yes, although—"

"Furthermore—"

Shaun couldn't take it any longer. He picked her up and slammed his mouth over hers and kissed her. Hard. Gem stood motionless for a moment before she relented, her arms rising to wrap around his neck. Their lips remained in contact as he smoothed his hands up her back, grapping hold of her ponytail so that eventually he could pull her away gently.

He didn't separate them for a good long time.

When he did, they stared into each other's eyes, and that deep sensation of being one person in two bodies hit again. Upsetting her made him ache inside. Happy and content was what he wanted, not this frustrated, volatile creature.

Shaun cleared his throat. "I assume you'd like me on my knees to grovel and ask for forgiveness?"

Gem fought from smiling. He saw it, the corner of her mouth twitched. Twice. "You are good in that position."

He snickered. "Dirty girl."

She let go of a little more of her rigid control. "I'm still mad at you."

Shaun fell to his knees. She shrieked as he clasped her hips and hauled her close. He buried his face against her belly, rubbing from side to side. "I was terribly mistaken. Forgive me."

A tug on his hair brought his gaze up to meet hers. "I don't want teriyaki muffins. Not even fluffy ones."

What the...?

She grinned outright. "Whatever you just said was muffled. I doubt you were really talking about indigestible breakfast food."

Shaun grabbed her hand and yanked, catching her by surprise. She fell without a sound and he caught her on his lap. He kissed her cheek then nuzzled the side of her face. "I'm sorry. Really. The only thing I have in my defense is that long line of southern bookings who freaked when they couldn't see an outhouse for miles."

"Ick. Okay, I kind of sympathize with them regarding that issue, but Shaun? I'm not everybody."

"You're right. You're not."

Gem tapped her long fingers on his arm. "If that's the usual you get, then I understand the whole 'insane' thing you were talking about better. I'm sorry I snapped at you, but really, I understood this project would take physical work."

Pride swelled inside him. "And I'm sorry I ever doubted you. We're going to work together, right?"

She nodded rapidly. "It's just another example, though, of me not feeling in control of my own life. I'm getting tired of it, Shaun."

"You stepped forward and took control damn well the day of the fight." He rearranged her so he could kiss her more easily, enjoying having her rest on his thighs.

The smile on her face lit the area. "I did, didn't I?"

He chuckled, and she hit her fists against his chest in mock anger. He caught her hands and kissed her fingers, making sure they made eye contact. He wanted the words to sink in deep. "Listen. I want you to do this. I know you can do this. I'm going to help you any way I can, and in the end you'll have everything you need to finish your research."

Gem smiled before eyeing him with suspicion. "Why did you decide to wait until now to have this discussion?"

*Oops.* "I didn't say anything before because..."

"You hoped I would give up, right?"

Busted. "Honest truth? At first, when we were back in Whitehorse, and even in Dawson? Yes, but for the last few days, no. I've discovered you're more than capable, but..." He stroked her fingers, sighing lightly. "I guess I'm guilty of wanting to protect you, when you don't really need it."

Comprehension lit her eyes. "That's what you were doing the other day, isn't it? You were keeping secrets about northern politics to protect me?"

Damn, she was good. Full-out confession seemed the only way to redeem himself. Shaun nodded slowly. "There is so much about the north that's wild and out of control—I was trying to make sure you saw the positive parts."

Gem wrinkled her nose. "Like bloody brawls in the streets?"

Shaun snorted. "I'm obviously not a very good spin doctor. In some cases, what you see is what you get."

She wiggled, and he set her free, rising to his feet as she paced over to the pile of camping equipment he had laid out. She stared at it for the longest time before turning. Her beautiful face was smooth, but there was a fire in her eyes he was coming to love. The stubborn determination that made his body squirm with desire as she made a decision that was all hers.

"Teach me."

He nodded as he stepped forward. "I can pack for us—"

"No, *teach* me." Gem caught him by the arm, and this time she pulled *him* against her body. "If I don't know how to do a task, I'm more than capable of learning how, but only if you trust me enough to let me try."

Something inside him got up on its feet and cheered. "I trust you."

She tugged off her sweater and folded it over the back of the chair. "So, what's the best way to get all our gear into the pack?"

A trickle of sweat ran down her back. How could it be this warm? They were in the north—the barren land should be cold, challenging. If they actually held a true Survivor contest somewhere other than where the women could wander beaches nearly naked, Gem had always imagined the event would take place in the north.

She really didn't want to be the one voted off the island today.

In front of her, Shaun slowed, waving a hand. She waved back and motioned him on.

Yesterday he'd given her lessons on packing. When he'd snuck the extra heavy objects into his own pack, she hadn't said a word. That kind of help she would accept, for a few days at least. No matter how many Pilates classes and P90X workouts she'd done, it wasn't the same as carrying all her possessions on her back.

Her boots were killing her.

There was no way she was going to tell him that.

Instead, she looked over the terrain, taking deep breaths of the clean air, following the narrow game trail Shaun had found that led in the direction of the birthing grounds. They had a week to get in and out. Plenty of time for her to take soil samples and gather all the other data she needed before they retreated to a distance to make observations while not disturbing the herd.

A week of camping out under a sky that remained light after midnight. Every step of the experience was a new adventure. Would the stars even appear? Would she be able to keep up physically?

Would she survive without running water and a flush toilet?

Shaun whistled, and she snapped her attention up to see him lower his pack and stretch his back. Another rest break—every one felt wonderful and every time it was a little more agonizing to pick up the pack again and start all over.

She pasted a smile on her face and focused on the things she *was* enjoying.

*I will not whine. I will not whine.*

"That's it for the day." Shaun reached to help her, dropping her pack to the ground and lowering his hands to her shoulders. The quick massage he gave felt so incredible it hurt.

"Really? No more hiking? It's still early." *Idiot!* What was she saying? Stopping now was a wonderful idea.

Shaun twisted her toward him, a wide grin splitting his face. "We need to set up camp, and the first couple days that will take longer."

Gem nodded. Logical, and a great excuse to boot. She leapt at it. "Tell me what to do."

She had practiced back home, but every tent was different. Shaun's was dome-shaped with long poles that arched and crisscrossed, and by the time they had three of them inserted in the straps of the main frame, she was totally confused as to which way she was supposed to turn and ended up zigging when she should have zagged. His solid torso connected with hers, and she teetered precariously before he grabbed on and held her upright.

Shaun didn't seem to mind she was a klutz. "We must stop meeting like this."

She attempted to untangle herself, but he trapped her, leaning down to press their lips together and kiss her tenderly. Warmth poured from him, and for a minute she forgot all about trying to make a good impression.

Kissing was so much fun. At least, with Shaun it was.

He licked her lower lip, tugged it lightly between his teeth before dipping back into her mouth with his tongue. Gem let go of the straps she'd been clinging to, instead, catching hold of his shoulders and keeping her balance by using his strength.

They would have continued for a lot longer if the wind hadn't chosen that moment to pick up and flap the loose edge of the tent.

Shaun slipped away. "Whoa, I'm not being a very good teacher. Make camp first, fool around second."

"Is that in the official rule book?" Gem followed his pointing finger and tugged the fabric until it settled into its proper place.

He laughed out loud. "Oh, darling, you can't ask me about anything official. I'm afraid the only reason I ever found out the rules was so I could break them."

Now that was just silly. "That's not true."

Shaun paused in the middle of unzipping the tent flaps. "Sure it is."

*Men.* Gem raised a brow. "So you didn't register our flight? And you don't do safety inspections on the helicopter?"

He sat back on his heels. "Of course not. I mean, of course I did. I mean..."

She giggled and he smiled sheepishly.

"See? Rules aren't all bad."

Shaun nodded. "I guess. I usually just do what I think is right. It's not always what others have in mind."

Gem settled on the rock he'd brought over for her. That sentiment wasn't as foreign an idea to her as he imagined. "I know you might not believe it, but I agree with you. At home when I disagreed, there were occasionally better ways to get what I wanted than out-and-out rebellion."

Shaun pulled out the rolled-up mattresses and set them to inflate on the floor of the tent. "You said your father wasn't pleased with you taking the trip north."

Gem sighed. "No."

"Then how did you manage to get the project approved?"

"Signed up without him knowing."

He squeezed her shoulder, approval in his tone. "Sneaky."

Guilt mixed with satisfaction. She was glad she'd done it, but... "Devious. Deceitful—"

"I like sneaky. Sneaky has its place." Shaun patted the ground beside him. "Come on, I'll show you how to link together our Therm-a-Rests and our sleeping bags. Then from now on that will be one of your chores when we make camp."

A burst of spontaneous joy hit. Gem wrapped her arms around him and squeezed as tight as she could. Her off-balance hug forced the two of them to tumble to the surface of the still uninflated mattresses.

Shaun laughed and kissed her nose. "What's that all about? Can't wait to jump me?"

*Hmm, yes.* But the sexual heat rolling through her veins was less intoxicating than the happiness spreading tiny tendrils that tangled all around her.

She *did* like learning new things, and trying new adventures, even if her feet throbbed like crazy. She rolled up on an elbow and smiled at him. "Thank you for escorting me on the trip. I'm glad I get to do this with you. Very glad."

His cheeky grin lit the whole tent.


The flames crackled, and Shaun added another branch, pushing the glowing embers together to make the coals flare upward with the extra fuel. The air around them was full of soft noises—the shifting of birds and small animals in the scattered brush. The gentle trickle of the creek running along the perimeter of the rise behind them.

The sound of a contented sigh as Gem relaxed at his side.

"You okay?" He'd been impressed. The entire hike she'd never once complained, even though he knew she had to be dying.

His princess had more steel in her spine than he'd ever expected.

Gem rested against him as they stared into the fire. "I've never done this before."

Shaun chuckled. "Not many people have. Which particular new experience is catching your attention?"

She tilted her head back, and the dark stars in her eyes twinkled. "It's bright daylight out and yet we're sitting by a fire. I always associate fires with darkness. Something to look at and fill your senses."

"Ahhh, but you're talking about southern fires. Here in the north, our fires are multisensory."

Gem wrinkled her nose. "Go on."

"Don't look with just your eyes. Look with all your senses. Then it won't matter that the sun is shining, you'll have the whole picture."

He settled her against the backrest he'd made, then reached to unlace her boots.

"What are you doing?" Light suspicion hovered in her eyes.

"Just relax. Check out the fire. I'm fixing your feet."

She leaned back, and as he pulled off the boot she groaned, a pure unadulterated sound of pleasure.

He worked the massage, pressing his thumbs into the arch

of her foot, smoothing the cream he'd grabbed over the places where her footwear had rubbed. She had fewer hot spots than he'd expected. He lifted her foot and examined it closer. A newbie hiker and no blisters? Impossible—the boots had to be more than two days old.

"You said you'd worn these boots around Whitehorse."

Gem cracked open an eye. "I did."

"These boots were broken in more than that."

She waved a hand in the air. "I just meant I'd worn them recently. Ever since I got approval for the project, I've been all over the estate grounds to do conditioning walks. I went out first thing in the morning before my father got up."

"Sneaky again. Well, you did great."

Her pleased expression warmed him. She relaxed and let him take care of her, and he enjoyed every second. Watching her face, seeing the minute responses to his touch. Then she took a big breath, staring up into the still-light sky.

"There are strange things done under the midnight sun..." she recited. "The poems make a lot more sense, having seen how light it really is."

Shaun grinned. "Robert Service. Now there was a man I could relate to."

She wiggled upright, wrapping her arms around her legs. "I read a bunch of his work in preparation for this trip. I enjoyed some of it, but the occasional bit that—"

A shiver shook her whole frame, and Shaun laughed. "Didn't like the part with the sizzling bonfire?"

She poked him. "No. Definitely not."

Shaun stared at her. The fire was dying down, but he didn't want to go to bed yet. She had to be sore, and there was one sure way to cure some of those aches.

His wolf pranced with excitement, nudging closer to the surface. Gem's smile faded slightly, changing to awe. He sensed her wolf wanted to come out as well. Wanted to meet his. They'd been denied for long enough.

"Gem?"

She swallowed hard. "I...I don't know why I'm feeling like this."

"It's our wolves. Don't you think it's time that they got to meet? Got some time to play?"

She nodded slowly.

"Changing will make your feet feel better. A couple shifts can help cure the little things like rising blisters and muscle aches." And he'd get to see her. See the colour of her fur and the way she moved—to appreciate how her human dignity and power would adapt as she shifted into her animal form.

He didn't want to wait any longer.

He rose, tugging her by the hand.

"Shaun—I don't know about this. I mean, yes, I know it would help, but..."

"What's wrong?"

"We don't shift very often back home. Special occasions only."

Shock socked him in the gut. "You're shitting me."

"Shaun!"

He was too surprised to apologize for his language. "Special occasions? I can understand not shifting outside where you could get shot, but really? Are you talking like once a month or only in formal settings? That's insane."

She tossed him a dirty look. "I thought we agreed that word was not allowed into this relationship."

"Gem, no matter what else we have to deal with, our wolves are the pair that need to be free, not formal."

She shook her hands in frustration. "I know that, but it's tough, okay? Changing on a casual basis is not what I'm used to."

He held her tight, resting his forehead against hers. They breathed slowly for a few minutes, the embers of the fire giving a final last gasp before fading away to nothing. Shaun didn't want to push, but damn it, this was not an issue he was willing to give on.

They were wolves. He would not deny that, and she shouldn't either.

Still, in the interest of attempting to not caveman her, he offered an out. "If you really don't want to, we can wait." He stroked her fingers lightly, thrilling at the smoothness under his fingertips. "But, Gem, I want to see your wolf. I want a chance to admire and run with you. To show you the north through your other eyes."

She clung to him for another moment before stepping back and squaring her shoulders. "I want that as well. To run with you."

He stripped, the entire time watching her take off her own clothing. It wasn't an erotic striptease, but every article she removed, folded and placed on the blanket added to the pressure building in his body.

His wolf snapped at him, reminding him sex would have to wait.

She was beautiful, standing naked in the twilight of the midnight sun. Then she shifted, and he smiled even harder. She was so tiny compared to the wolves of the north. Dainty, delicate.

So Gem.

He squatted and held out his arms. "You're just as beautiful as I thought you'd be."

She strolled over slowly, her nose wiggling like crazy. All the different scents of the north—it must be like a smorgasbord to her. His hand brushed her head, and she stilled, letting him stroke her from nose to back.

When he tugged at her front paw, she sat, head tilted to the side as he caressed her.

"So elegant, fragile almost—"

Gem leaned against him, hard, until she'd pushed him to the ground. She planted both front paws on his chest and growled as she stared into his eyes.

Okay, ix-nay on the fragile bit. He laughed, wiggling to free himself and cursed instead as a twig dug into his bare backside. "Hey, no fair. Fine, you're not delicate. You're a Viking. An Amazon. The most incredible example—*oof.*"

She lay on top of him, her meager weight still enough to make him feel each and every rock poking into his back.

Gem lowered her nose to the crook of his neck and sniffed, her teasing growl changing to one of satisfaction. Shaun trembled as he fought to maintain control, but he couldn't hold back his wolf any longer.

He rolled as he changed, the sensation of limbs and bones transitioning from human to wolf in one easy flow. There was an almost erotic pleasure in the shift, and as he came up on his feet, knowing his mate waited for him made it even better.

She'd rolled with him, finding a safe spot to rest as he stood and took a deep breath in through his nose. If he'd thought she smelled good before, the aroma was nothing compared to now. The extra strength of his wolf nose not only thrilled at their connection, but was ecstatic to find they shared a scent. Shaun threw back his head and howled in delight.

From a distance, a series of long and short yips answered him, and he grinned. Those weren't shifters—just natural wolves, but it was always exciting to be able to appreciate a good songfest.

Gem sat silently, staring at him.

Was it too much? The unfamiliarity of the change now, or was it that this was the first time their wolves had met? He walked over and nudged her, stroking her side. Silky soft, there was no other way to describe her. Shaun wrapped himself around her and finished by resting his head along her back, the wolf equivalent of a hug.

She wiggled, and he rose to allow her freedom. Once she was on her feet, she shook then walked up to the highest ridge overlooking their camp. She waited, one paw landing on the trail, before pulling back.

Shaun understood. He stepped past her, making sure to brush her as he went by. Then he picked up the pace and ran. It wasn't a race, but it was far quicker than they'd traveled in human form. The intriguing scents of the night crossed and crisscrossed their path. A covey of ptarmigan. The trickle of the stream much louder as they approached. There had been arctic hare in the area not even an hour ago by their lingering scent signature, and for a moment he considered tracking one down just for the fun of seeing what Gem would do when they spooked it up.

No, no threatening to do something bloody just to freak her out. That was totally immature and not how he was to treat his mate.

There was a crash behind him, and Shaun spun in time to see Gem's backside disappear between two low bushes. He followed, paws light on the spongy turf of the tundra, scattered rocks lying in flat slabs below bushes that would be waist high on him in human form.

It made a dandy maze for his wolf, so he ignored everything but Gem's scent.

A scream rang out, and he doubled his speed, bursting into a clearing in time to see Gem holding down a rather bloody hare.

She licked her muzzle then swiped it clean with her free paw, pushing a few strands of fur back into place.

Shaun chuckled and paced forward. The tilt to her head said it all. She totally expected him to be shocked she'd made a kill.

Well, he was. But that was beside the point. He was also tickled that she'd proven to be far more than a princess in lilywhite gloves.

He crouched in front of Gem, his tail doing all kinds of doglike things. Letting it pound into the dirt was undignified, but he simply couldn't help it. And when she nosed the carcass in his direction, gifting him with the bunny, he sang again with satisfaction.

While the whole mystical wolf-mate thing might be out of his hands, it was good to discover that his wolf was one hundred and fifty percent in love.

And his human side? Not that far behind.

The Moonshine Pub remained crowded, minutes away from closing. Caroline knew all of them were wolves. They would simply take the party over to the pack house, and keep drinking and fooling around until the wee hours of the night.

One of Evan's more persistent admirers was hanging all over him again. The outfit covering the woman was strategically arranged to ensure maximum legal exposure. A sour taste slicked Caroline's tongue—the bitch was one of the pack who enjoyed making trouble and watching others clean it up.

The perfect opportunity had finally arrived. Evan wanted to know if she could handle being linked with him? Sex, along with the rest of it?

She'd start with *the rest of it*—and it appeared a little violence was on the agenda. Fine. All those years of training hadn't been for nothing. She might lack wolf reflexes, but a third-level black belt and her stepfather's instruction counted for a lot when facing someone who *only* had being a wolf on her side.

Caroline removed her jacket to cut down on loose objects for the other woman to grab. She tossed it over a nearby chair and shook her hands to loosen up.

It took a minute to weave her way through the crowd to the main bar. Evan sat on a tall stool, his back to the counter. He spotted her, his gaze following her approach. There was a bit of a challenge on his face. A dare. He was looking forward to her attempt, was he?

He'd better be damn well prepared for what she had on the agenda for later.

She lost sight of him as Ms. Trouble crawled between them, pressing her overflowing bosom tight to Evan's chest. Caroline shouldered past the groupies clustered around Evan and the bar. The fact she was totally surrounded by people who could change into wolves barely made her pause.

This had to be done.

She reached out and tapped the woman's bare shoulder. "You mind getting your paws off him?"

The heavy dye job in front of her—covering blonde, perhaps?—rotated oh-so-slowly as the brunette eased off Evan's lap. Caroline caught a quick glimpse of Evan's face, then he was blocked from sight again.

Bastard was enjoying this.

The theatrical posturing of the woman was for effect—only the intimidation factor was short-circuited by her rapid glances around the room to see if anyone was paying attention.

*Buzzzz.* Mistake number one. Don't take your eyes off the enemy.

Caroline considered giving a second warning, but since her opponent was a wolf, having the upper hand could be the deciding factor in the fight. She snatched a thick handful of the woman's hair and yanked. At the same time, Caroline slammed an arm forward, smacking the other woman's shoulder.

The brunette spun in a half-circle before throwing out her hands to catch her balance. The bar cleared around them. Caroline used her free hand to catch hold of one wrist and shove it behind the wolf's back. Using her full body weight, Caroline smashed them both forward against the suddenly empty counter.

Her opponent was pinned in one place, crying out in pain.

"I don't think you heard me. I would very much appreciate if you'd not drool all over Evan in the future." Caroline tightened her hold, all her attention on the woman. Waiting for her response.

When it came, she was ready. The brunette rocked her head back, attempting a head butt. Caroline ducked to the side and pushed the other woman's arm as high as possible without breaking it.

If Caroline had been watching the wolves circling them, she would have been knocked unconscious. Mistake number two on dye-job's part—Caroline knew protocol. No one would dream of interrupting this kind of dominance fight without backlash from the entire pack. Until the brunette was incapacitated on the floor, or Caroline was, this was between the two of them.

When her head failed to connect, the brunette snarled in frustration. "Pitiful little human. You can't be serious. He needs a wolf like me to be satisfied."

Caroline mock gasped. "Oh, you're a wolf? Sorry, I totally missed that. You being so weak and all."

A sudden burst of energy freed the woman, and Caroline found herself facing a very pissed-off opponent. The brunette flipped her hair back, seemingly ignorant her breasts were one millimeter away from bursting free from her low-slung top. "Don't make me laugh. You can't expect to win a fight against me. You're ugly too."

Caroline snorted her disbelief. "Ugly? That's as good as you can give? Chemically enhanced, silicon-stuffed, socially inept Luddite."

The brunette's jaw hung open. Then she moved.

It was scary exactly how quick wolves were. Caroline was ready, but not fast enough, and the woman's first blow landed. Wincing in pain, Caroline ducked, swinging out her leg to kick the other woman's knees. As she fell, Caroline rose to come crashing down on top, adding her weight to the full-body slam. The woman went wild, elbows flailing, hands moving constantly. One blow smacked into Caroline's eye, one landed on her chest just below her neck.

If the fight went on too long, Caroline knew she'd be out of luck. She had to end it quickly or all her plans would be shot.

So she fought dirty. Grabbed the woman's hair and slammed her head against the ground. When the body under her bucked hard enough to nearly throw her off, Caroline hooked her legs around the brunette's waist and wrestled that arm back up again.

She didn't stop pushing this time until she heard a sharp crack.

A sudden scream of pain cut through the noise and the entire bar went silent. The cheers and catcalls of encouragement faded as a pair of dusty-coloured shoes appeared in Caroline's peripheral vision.

Evan.

His hand touched her shoulder. "Let her go."

The woman sniffled softly as her friends helped her up. There were no heated glances backward, no veiled threats. Instead, the brunette shuffled away, cradling her injured arm. Caroline had won the fight fair and square, and there was only one thing left to do.

Evan held her elbow and lifted her to her feet. She kept her head high, making eye contact with as many of the pack as she could. Some faces showed admiration, some confusion. Curiosity grew by the second as Caroline finished her slow pivot to come face to face with their Alpha.

His dark eyes twinkled. "Don't like her touching me?"

*Final test.* "I don't share."

Her words triggered an explosion of sound as all the voices swelled again with questions. Shouts. Then the noise disappeared, drowned in the rush of blood in her ears as Evan tugged her against him and took her lips. Right there in front of the entire pack, his warmer-than-human body pressed tight to hers. He lifted one hand to support her head, the other planted in the scoop of her back to control her.

It wasn't just the heat, it was his kiss. The kiss she'd dreamed about ever since setting eyes on the shifter. There was only physical attraction between them, but *only* was pretty damn incredible. With their mouths fused together, his tongue explored and teased. Demanded a response, and, oh man, she gave it. She clung to his shoulders, buried both hands in his hair. Things grew a little foggy, but she might have lifted one leg and wrapped it around the back of his thigh. The reaction of his body was very clear, and very solid, and she canted her hips to make sure she stayed in contact with the bit of solid because it felt So. Damn. Good.

That's about when she remembered they were still in the bar. Surrounded by the pack. Who had once again fallen silent.

She was really messing with their wolfie minds tonight, wasn't she?

Evan eased off the kiss, his left hand smoothing over her leg, her ass, then back to cradle her thigh. He slowly lowered the limb, keeping them in close contact until she stood before him again. Only now her lips were swollen, her heart racing more than when she'd been in the midst of the fight.

He stared at her, approval the clearest emotion. Desire right behind it. He dug in his back pocket for keys, tossing them to someone without losing eye contact with her.

"Bar is closed. Everyone, have a great evening. I know I'm going to."

Then he scooped her into his arms and carried her out.

# Chapter Twelve

"Think you'll be finished today?"

Gem laid the final vial in the padded carrying case and closed it carefully. "Definitely. I've taken my last set of samples, and if you give me a little more time for a few more pictures, we're done."

Shaun nodded, squeezed her shoulder and headed back toward their campsite.

She turned to watch him.

The past week had been incredible. Three easy days of hiking had brought them to the birthing grounds, and every step of the way Shaun had taught her something new. Dealing with experiences in the wilds had been night and day different than her practice runs back in the lab, but he'd been patient and playful all at the same time.

Gem packed away the last of her supplies and tucked them into the small bag that attached to her main pack. Wandering back to the campsite, she took pictures. Not ones for her studies, more to help her remember the time she'd spent with Shaun. A shot of where he'd taught her how to light the tiny white gas stove. They'd cooked supper using a dehydrated meal pack, and it had actually been edible. Another of the once-again pristine spot where he'd demonstrated how to build a small fire and leave no trace.

Where she'd made a primitive latrine—okay, that one she didn't take a picture of. Some things were better left to the imagination.

She made the final approach to their campsite to discover him lying flat out in the tent, his feet sticking through the open flaps of the door.

"Lazybones." Gem gave his ankle a gentle kick. She lowered her bag to the ground as she squatted to peek in at him.

"Hmm, you called?" His boots rotated, and she squeaked as he shot out a hand and pulled her on top of him. "You want to be lazy with me?"

Gem wiggled, widening her knees to get comfortable. "I'm ready to break camp when you are."

"That's not relaxing."

She placed her hands on top of his chest and arranged herself so she could stare into his eyes. He was laughing again, but she didn't feel as if she were being insulted anymore. "I'm sorry, Mr. Stevens, were you saying that you'd like to stay out here longer? Did you miss the part of the contract that said you were required to not only get me into the wilderness, but out?"

He raised a brow. "That wasn't in the contract I read."

Gem punched him lightly. "You."

"But just think about the possibilities." Shaun crossed his arms behind his head and let out a huge sigh. Contentment rolled off him. "I think we should go back to the land. Go bush. You want to give up civilization and just move into the wilderness? I know this great—"

She slapped a hand over his mouth, blocking the words. "Thank you, no. I've enjoyed the trip, but I'm not quite ready for this as a permanent state of affairs."

Shaun licked her palm, and she sat up with a grimace. He

smiled. "You make the best faces. And I mean that as a compliment. I know exactly if I'm in shit or deep shit when I look at you."

Fighting to keep from smiling, Gem folded her arms and considered how incredible she felt—far more relaxed than expected. Even his swearing seemed normal and nothing to fuss over.

She wasn't sure that was a good thing or not.

"Then what does my face tell you right now?" She imagined sitting in the Jacuzzi tub on the balcony of her bedroom back home, with Shaun at her side. Warm water surrounding them, icy cold drinks in their hands—the sound of the river as it swept against the shore a rumble in the background.

Shaun froze, lifting one finger against her lips. He whispered, "Do you hear that?"

Impossible. Had he really connected with her vision? "You heard the river?"

He shook his head, the words a hint above a whisper. "More like a waterfall."

Shaun twisted, pointing toward the side of the tent and Gem cocked her head to listen better. Oh my, he was right. There was a steady ribbon of water pouring out to the north. Only, there were no water sources that direction, and there was the distinct smell of...urine?

*Ugh. What?*

A snort sounded from the east, and Shaun swore. "This is not good. This is so not good."

It took a minute to untangle themselves, both trying to remain as silent as possible. Gem wiggled as he sat up until finally they faced the front of the tent.

"Do you see anything?" she asked. Talking in hushed tones

just seemed proper.

"Smell."

Gem took a deep breath through her nose and recognition hit. While the first and strongest scent was her and Shaun, the biggest one after that was something she hadn't expected. Through the narrow gap in the unzipped fly, she watched in horror as the hairy but slender legs of a caribou wandered past.

They were here? Already?

"Shaun. Oh...drat." Gem shuffled forward to take a cautious peek. The herd had arrived. "They aren't supposed to be *here*. And they shouldn't be anywhere near this far north for a week."

"Something sped them up?"

She blew out a long slow breath. "We have to leave, now."

Shaun touched her arm lightly. "If you didn't notice, we're trapped. You really think leaving is a good idea?"

Gem held out a hand toward him. "Let me take a better look, okay? If this is the leading edge, we might have a chance."

"What—?"

Ignoring his grip on her arm, Gem slipped through the tent fly and stood as slowly as she could.

Caribou surrounded them as far as the eye could see. The pregnant females, the yearling calves following their dames. An ear twitched in her direction, a couple of heads swiveled. Silence hung in the air for a moment until it was broken by the buzz of a fly and the call of a bird.

Then the entire herd ignored her as the animals went back to nibbling on the sparse June growth.

There was a gentle tug on her pant leg. "I swore I wouldn't use the word insane again, but I'm very, very tempted."

Gem twisted slowly to smile down at him. "Trust me, it's

okay. Are you hungry?"

His grimace was hilarious. "Um, Gem, protected animal. You want to go hunting again, I'll take you out for more bunnies later, okay?"

"Silly. Are you hungry, as in—if you're not we can get out of this. We'll have to abandon the tent."

Complete concentration replaced his earlier concern. "You're talking about shifting?"

Gem nodded. "We can walk amongst the caribou in our wolf forms. As long as we're not hunting, they won't care. It will spook them less than if we make the attempt as humans."

"Even with the pregnant cows?"

There was a risk. "They're a lot more skittish right now, yes, but I still think our wolves would be the best."

He was already removing his boots. "Then get naked, woman."

She took another slow glance around as she lowered herself back into the protection of the tent. The herd had come in on a more northern route than she'd expected. Shaun was right. Something must have spooked them to make them go off course this far, but then animals' movements never were completely predictable. It wasn't as if the yearly migration followed a set road.

As she shrugged off her coat, Shaun reached to help her. His touch distracted her more than simple assistance required. She wiggled in protest. "Timing is everything."

Warmth crowded against her back as he snuck her shirt from her shoulders and cuddled up close, their naked torsos in contact. "I agree. We don't really have to leave this exact moment, do we?"

*Tempting, but no.* Gem mustered her meager reserves and

twisted away. "We do. Because the goal is to not rile up the herd any more than necessary. If we start fooling around, they'll be traumatized for sure by your screaming."

She tugged off her pants and folded them out of habit before she realized he'd gone dead quiet. Turned to stare into a very wide smile.

"Why, Ms. Jacobs, I do believe you just suggested offering me sex scandalous enough to cause me to scream."

She kept her gaze fixed on his. "I believe, sir, what I insinuated is that was the status quo..."

Their whole conversation was held at a mere whisper, but the sense of joy spilling through her was powerful enough to make her feel as if they'd been shouting at the top of their voices. They grinned at each, and satisfaction rose higher.

"Thank you."

He lifted a brow. "For screaming?"

"For believing me. For trusting me about the caribou."

Even naked, when Shaun tipped his head, he was as elegant as any of the suitors she'd had back home during formal regattas and society dinners. "Your lead, my lady."

Shifting was always miraculous. Erotic sensations trickled through her, powerful and strong. Not only her limbs changed, but her thoughts, as her wolf rose closer to the surface. She was still Gem, but more. The wolf was real, and honest. Painfully honest—her other half wondered when they were going to get around to the marking business. She wanted permanent proof of her mate.

Gem ignored the canine hussy's questions and rolled to her feet. She bumped against Shaun's larger body as he completed his shift. They stroked each other with chin and cheeks for a moment, enjoying the contact between their furry forms.

Then she stuck her nose out the tent flaps again, sniffing lightly. She wanted to let her new, more wolfish scent slowly carry on the air as a warning. That would be the least intrusive method to announce their presence.

Shaun sneezed and the herd swiveled their focus.

*Fudge.* So much for waiting. Gem took a cautious step forward. Then another. Head held high, body erect.

This wasn't a hunting gait, she was taking a simple stroll through the tundra. A half-dozen paces brought her within lunging distance of one of the huge caribou. These weren't the smaller southern herbivores that lived in Georgia. Like all northern animals, these were larger, bulkier. Built for the cold and danger of the north.

The creature could kick her brains out with one well-executed thrust. Gem stood motionless for a long time.

The caribou transferred its weight, then went back to grazing.

She breathed a sign of relief before heading up the trail toward the helicopter. They would have to stay in wolf for a while. Wait for the herd to finish moving past.

They'd been in the wrong place at the wrong time, but as she worked her way slowly through the now-crowded landscape, Shaun beside her, Gem took in everything she could. The data might not be able to be reported and documented the same as if she were in human form, but talk about first-hand information. She counted pregnant cows, made a close-up inspection of the animals' coats after the long winter.

There were no words to describe her emotions. This was the pinnacle of her research, albeit not how she'd envisioned it. In wolf form, with a mate by her side?

She couldn't imagine how her life could get any better.

Shaun nudged her lightly, his furry shoulder far higher than hers.

They moved together away from the herd.

Shaun had seen a lot of things during his years in the north, many awe-inspiring. Standing on the summit of a mountain, staring over the tips of the neighbouring peaks as the sun painted the crags with gold and crimson. The skies over Haines filled with enormous bald eagles as they congregated each November. He'd experienced heart-pounding excitement as they'd shot the Tatashini River in kayaks, marveled at the moon-like landscape at the top of White Pass.

None of those situations had ever made him feel like he did right now. Because even with friends along, they'd been a side component to the event. This, being with Gem, *was* the event. It was so much richer and more—real.

As if he'd been dreaming all his life, but now that she'd woken him up he could truly live.

It took only a few minutes to leave the main mass of the pack. There were stragglers ranging farther out though, so Gem led them until they were far downwind. Her path brought them upward, where they could look back over where they'd come. She sat, staring for a minute then shifted. He followed her lead, the cool breeze carrying the scent of the herd straight toward them.

"I think we're okay." Gem pointed to the side where their tent was surrounded. "But we might not be able to get back to our gear for a day or two. They've settled in—there's no telling if they will move on as quickly or sit here for a bit before they decide it's time to make another push."

"They don't smell as if they're upset."

She nodded, crossing her arms over her chest as she

shivered lightly. "We got out in time."

Shaun tucked her into his embrace. Hmm, it felt marvelous to have her there. He nuzzled her hairline. "We're going to have to share body heat."

An extremely un-Gemlike response escaped her.

He twisted her to face him and gave her a mock dirty look. "Did you just snort at me?"

Gem planted her fists on her hips. Naked, that looked good on her. Come to think of it, everything looked good on her, especially while naked.

"Shaun, did you miss the part that we're now stranded on the side of a hill, no clothes, no food. No idea when we're going to be able to get back to our supplies. And you want to have sex?"

He thought real hard. Was this a trick question? "Yup, that about covers it."

The sound started deep inside her before rumbling upward. A snort? A giggle? It soon changed into rolling laughter, quiet enough to not disturb the herd, but unmistakable and unstoppable.

And contagious. He couldn't resist joining her, amusement bubbling up and making his heart light. They could make it through this, and more than simply come out okay, they would rock it. No matter what had to happen down the road, they were meant to be together.

He checked a grassy spot on the ground, moving aside pokey objects before he sat on his bare butt. Then he pulled her into his lap and cradled her close until her body stopped shaking.

She wiped tears from her eyes, her dazzling smile making him happy inside. "Thank you."

"Anytime. You gonna share what set you off, love?"

Gem used his shoulders to brace herself, lifting and rearranging until she straddled him. "Just you being you. Sincere, but blunt. I find I like that, Shaun Stevens. I like you, a lot."

She snuck in closer, pressing her naked breasts to his chest. Her fingers slipped into his hair, and she brought their mouths together for a long, slow kiss, fires rising between them in an instant.

That wasn't the only thing rapidly rising.

He tore himself away, hating to leave the warmth of her lips but needing to before things got out of hand. "Gem, if you don't want to have sex, we need to stop—holy crap, woman."

She'd lifted her hips and rubbed the thickening length of his erection with her sex. Moisture and heat coated him. He cupped her ass in his hands and helped her make another pass.

"Did I answer your question?" she whispered in his ear a second before she nipped the tip of his earlobe.

Shaun's heart pounded, each pulse echoed at the base of his spine. His cock was harder than he'd remembered, wanting more than just the tease of her body.

*Down, boy, not yet.*

He hoisted her far enough her breasts were presented like beautiful gifts for him to savour. A gentle lick to prime the tip before he wrapped his lips around one peak and sucked hard, pulling a gasp from Gem. Her hips pulsed against his belly, the crown of his erection feeling the heat of her core like a treasure. Lowering her an inch let him slip his cock head between her wet folds, and still maintain mouth contact with her nipples.

Almost perfect. He let go of her hips to cup her breasts

more easily, alternating sides with kisses and attention until her wiggling became too much and he couldn't wait any longer.

She pulled back and stared into his eyes as she lowered herself onto his shaft, sinking to the root.

His brain went ninety-nine percent numb. The last tiny portion still working lit celebratory firecrackers.

Incredible sensations floated over him. The pleasure of her body wrapped tight around his, the heat radiating form her torso, heavy breasts filling his hands. She moved, undulating up and down in a slow, steady rhythm as he fought to keep from coming in three seconds flat.

Then she brought their mouths together again, and her tongue danced against his, shaking him to the core. It was more than a kiss. More than sex. Much more than simply another incredible experience in the wilderness.

It was heaven on earth, and he'd found the secret entrance.

Gem nipped at his bottom lip, and he smiled. Hands tight on her hips, he picked up the pace. "You looking for some biting, sweetheart?"

Another nip, this time to his ear again. He'd never been one for letting the girls play with his ears before, and now he knew why.

He'd been saving them for Gem, because *holy fucking moly*, did it ever feel good.

She sucked the tingling lobe into her mouth and slammed their hips together harder. "I'm not ready to mark you, but damn if I don't want to nibble you all over."

Sadness crept in, just a tiny bit. She was right though. They'd agreed to wait until they had all their cards lined up. "Okay. Biting is fine. No marking, just—shit!"

She dragged her teeth down his neck and his cock grew two

inches. Or more.

"Hmm, you like that, do you?"

"Didn't think my southern lady had teeth."

She nipped again, and he wasn't able to stop himself. He pounded into her, cock driving hard. Fastened his mouth on her neck and sucked for all he was worth. If he couldn't officially mark her, he was damn well going to leave his signature another way.

She canted her hips slightly, and his groin rubbed across her mound. With a twist, he slipped his hand between their bodies and pressed on her clit. She threw back her head and screamed, choking off in mid-cry.

He would have laughed in delight if at that moment the freight train hadn't hit him as well, release exploding out as his cock jerked deep inside her. Pleasure rose in waves that blurred his vision and drained all logic from his brain.

Fuck, *fuck.* Wowity fuck.

Sweaty and sticky and happy and mind-fuddled, they clung together, kissing and caressing until the heat of their joining cooled enough they could both sit upright without using each other as a brace.

"I think you just killed me." Shaun nuzzled the side of her neck where there was a nice big hickey.

His wolf gloated with happiness.

"You talk pretty good for a dead guy."

"You know if I'm dead, you have to haul my carcass with you to the shores of Lake Laberge and cremate me." Shaun grinned as she slipped her hands around his neck and gave him one final kiss.

She pulled back and batted her lashes. "No. I'm not going to listen to you sizzle as you burn, thank you. Instead, I will be forced to weep copious amounts of tears while I pile rocks on your body and leave you here where the little animals will chew on your remains and continue the circle of life."

*Impressive.* "Is that your sweet innocent role-play persona? Because, like, I totally thought you meant that."

"I did mean it." Gem patted his cheek then rose off him, her warmth disappearing far too quickly and making him sad. She stretched and his mouth watered again. Hmm, how long was it possible to survive naked in the Alaskan wilderness if they had sex non-stop?

She was a researcher. Maybe she'd go for finding out.

Shaun glanced around. Below them, the herd had settled in, and he doubted there was any way they could get back to the tent for at least a day.

"Okay, love. Time to make a decision. You want to hang out for the next few days in our wolf skins?" She rotated to face him, the sky-blue background a stark contract with her dark skin. He dragged his gaze off her full breasts, forcing himself to focus on the current discussion. "Food and shelter would be a snap—it's not a bad solution. We can keep track of the beasts and gather our things as soon as they leave."

Gem hesitated. "Is there another option? I enjoyed my time as a wolf, but...I'm not sure I'm ready for more."

Shaun stood to take her hand. "How about this? We shift to run back to the chopper. In our wolves it should be around four hours. I've got an emergency stash there—everything we need to return to civilization for a few days. Once my sources tell us the herd has moved on, we'll come back and retrieve our things."

Gem gazed at their campsite. "You're not worried about abandoning our supplies?"

"Nah. The only thing that could cause a mess is the food, and it's all tucked away in bear-proof containers. What about your notes and research?"

"All safely packed up." She brought his hand to her mouth and kissed his knuckles. "I'd feel more comfortable with that plan. If you don't mind."

Shaun hurried to reassure her. "Don't feel bad you don't want to live wild for a few days. There are a lot of wolves who grew up in the Yukon who have never done an extended trip in wolf form."

Gem nodded. "May...maybe someday. I'm not sure, but I think I'd like to. Someday."

The fluttering sensation in his heart—was that a heart attack about to happen? Or the realization she had just implied they'd be together for long enough for there to be a someday? Even staying in the north?

Shaun tugged her to face him. He had to say it. "Gem—I want you to know..."

"We need to be going, right?" Gem stepped back, antsy. Nervousness surrounded her. "I'm starting to get hungry, and we need to be far away from the herd when that happens. I mean, if the wind changed right now, it would be terrible. You lead the way, okay?"

She shifted before he could respond. Before he could find out why all of a sudden she'd gone from sounding as if she had offered him the moon to shaking the dust from her feet as she fled.

She waited in wolf, tail twitching. Body shivering. He would go insane wondering what was wrong. Nothing physically had changed in the last few minutes. He must have said something to offend her, and the idea stabbed him in two.

*"Gem?"*

He thought at her as hard as possible. Nothing.

He shifted to wolf, moved to her side and held himself still. Breathing slowly, willing her to calm down. In spite of what he'd done to upset her, he wanted her to know how much he cared.

When she finally relaxed and licked his muzzle once, a tentative touch, he blew out a long breath. Whatever bullet had just passed, he was going to be very careful until he knew what was going on in that complicated head of hers.

They headed toward the chopper, two-plus days of hiking as humans eaten up under their much faster wolf gait. After two hours of travel, they'd already covered more than half the distance back. The still-illuminated sky helped as well, and other than the occasional side trip to nab a snack, they made good time.

Somewhere in the middle of the night they arrived. They were both tired, turning the corner into the clearing where they'd left the helicopter. Shaun was sure sleep was Gem's only focus. It was pretty much the only thing on his mind as well.

Which was why he didn't see the trap until it was too late.

# Chapter Thirteen

A sudden *snap* rang out, followed by the scream of a rope through a pulley. Gem's eyes, which had been closing in near sleep, flew open. Her hind left paw lifted in the air, caught in something, and she scrambled away, rolling to the right as hard as she could, all her senses waking up in a hurry.

The wolf that was Shaun howled, and she glanced upward to see him wrapped in a net like a fly in a spider's web. He warned her to hide, the simple communication they used in their wolf forms enough to get that message across loud and clear. She didn't bolt into the cover of the low-lying brush, instead dropping to her belly and lowering her head.

The scents on the air and the sounds reaching her ears told the story. There were bear shifters in the area. Their aroma seemed vaguely familiar as their human voices drew closer. She scrambled back, staying low to the ground, hiding where she could keep an eye on Shaun.

"Yoo-hoo, sweet lady. Lovely to finally meet you in person. You've led us on quite the trip." A voice rang out from the right as one of the shifters came into view. A Coleman lantern hung from his hand, brightening the twilight until he and his two companions were easily visible. "You may as well change, Gem. You're going to be with us for a while, and you'll be much more comfy in your human form."

"Didn't expect she'd travel in her wolf, Bruce. That's not what the report suggested."

"Where's the guide?"

"The guide is right here, you asshats." Shaun shifted, clutching the netting to pull himself to vertical in the wiggling trap. "What the hell do you think you're doing? Let me down."

"Shit, caught the wrong one." The skinniest of the three bear shifters came over to stand beside the net, his head level with Shaun's butt.

"Don't worry about it, Vince, she wouldn't go anywhere without him." Bruce stared at the scrub, his gaze passing within a few feet of where Gem lay hidden. "And we're not leaving without her."

"So we're at an impasse?" the third bear asked.

Bruce turned, his voice lowering. "You're not going to start that business again, are you? I thought I told you two no more quoting from *The Princess Bride* or I'd rip your fucking ears off."

"It's not my fault this time," Vince whined. "Norm started it."

"Sorry, Bruce." Norm crossed his hand over his heart then pressed a finger to his lips. "Not another word."

Gem locked her jaw together to stop from whimpering in fear. Shaun spun in a slow circle, the net he was caught in suspended from a cross post that had been attached to the airstrip's wind-kite tower. The bears had set a trap?

Bruce paced a step closer to Shaun. "Where's the lady?"

"I killed her and left her body for the crows." Shaun jerked the ropes harder.

*What?*

"Idiot! You know how the hell much she was worth?" Norm smacked a fist into Shaun's back. A harsh grunt escaped

199

Shaun as he attempted to twist away.

"Stop it, he's bullshitting us." Vince blocked another kidney punch from landing. "There's no reason for him to kill her."

"That's what you think," Shaun growled. "You didn't have to deal with her highness in the backcountry. Now let me down."

His insults slipped off like she was a duck who had fallen into the Takhini Hot Springs. He was trying to pull a fast one, and she needed to trust him. And help him.

And get them both out of this mess.

Bruce grabbed the net, stopping its steady swing. He twisted the trap until Shaun faced him.

"You're lying through your teeth. I can smell her on you— hmm, you're a little taken with the lady. Trying to move up in the world, wolf-boy?"

Shaun glared down at him. "What do you want with Gem?"

"Just doing a job. We caught wind of her arrival the minute she landed in Whitehorse. I hear her family is loaded. There are things we need to do in the next while that require cash. You do the math."

Gem froze. They were using her to get money? This wasn't happening. How had she gone from a simple-research-project/spread-her-wings outing to finding her mate and being used as a pawn?

She was not going to let this happen.

Shaun shrugged. "Good luck on that. The finding-her bit, I mean. She's a wolf, she can shift and go a lot faster than you bears, especially since she knows the territory better than you now. It will be days before you even spot her." He never glanced her way once, but she'd gotten the message. She could go back to the tent, she could hide and get away—it was true.

But like...*hell*...was she was going to leave him.

Her mate continued, total indifference in his voice as he baited the bears. "When I don't call in for the final stages of our flight on time, there will be all kinds of people and pack searching for us. You really don't want to be doing this."

"No, I really do," Bruce insisted. "We need the money, and see, your little scenario with us chasing her for days? Not going to happen. Because I bet she's watching right now."

*Fudge.*

Bruce examined the bush again, his lantern held high in the air. "You want to make this easy, Gem? Come on in, and we'll go ahead with the next step of the game plan."

"She's not stupid. You confessed you planned to kidnap her. Why the fuck should she be willing to come out?" Shaun rearranged himself awkwardly.

"You're right. Fine. Lower him, boys."

Vince's idea of letting him down consisted of whipping out a fixed blade knife and slashing the supporting rope in two. Shaun smacked the ground with a crash, a few choice swear words escaping.

Gem didn't move. Not when they pulled the ropes from Shaun and yanked him to his feet. Not when Norm and Vince grabbed him by the arms, forcing him forward to stand naked and defenseless before their boss. Not when Bruce placed the lantern at his feet.

Bruce called out louder. "Right. Of course she's not stupid. Gem, it's you we want. If you come with us now, your lover doesn't get the shit beat out of him. Simple."

He spun and planted a right hook into Shaun's belly. Fist meeting flesh was stomach-retching sickening. So was the expression on Shaun's face. He'd turned cold, cruel. As if her

Shaun wasn't there anymore.

Bruce bashed him again, across the jaw. Shaun's head snapped back with a crack, blood dripping from the side of his mouth. Another blow landed, and another. Shaun struggled against the bears restraining him. He lifted his legs and slammed them at Bruce. The bear shifter laughed as he ducked aside and struck repetitively.

He spoke between blows. "And, Shaun? If you decide to change to your wolf in the hopes you can escape us that way? Just remember a human body is a lot harder to hide. I have no trouble killing a wolf in an instant."

Gem hesitated. Maybe she wasn't supposed to cave. Maybe Shaun had some master plan up his sleeve, but witnessing his torture? She couldn't do it. There had to be a better solution.

She shifted back to human, crouched low. If they made a run for her, she would change again and escape. "Stop."

Shaun spoke, the first sound from him other than grunts of pain since the beating began. "Insane."

She wasn't going to fall for it—he'd said that on purpose, just to piss her off. Bruce pivoted, the lamplight at his feet smearing the smile on his face into a hideous caricature. "There's the lovely girl. Come on, dear. So nice of you to join us."

"You have to promise not to hurt Shaun anymore. He's my mate. He's worth money as well."

The sudden silence in the clearing was deafening.

"Your mate. Damn, that makes a huge difference." Bruce slapped Shaun on the shoulder. "You hound dog. Well done. I was joking before about moving up in the world, but you really did it."

"Shut your fucking face." Shaun's comment was greeted by

a punch to the back of his head from Vince, and her mate fell to his knees as the goons on either side of him released his arms.

"Shaun." Gem ran forward. The bad guys had all the reason they needed to not kill Shaun and leave his body behind. Either they took her word about the money or they would simply kill them both at some point. She figured she and Shaun had a better chance of surviving this adventure if they were together.

Bruce stepped aside and let her wrap an arm around Shaun.

"You weren't supposed to do this." Shaun held her hand as she helped him stagger to his feet.

"I thought you'd figured out by now I don't always do what I'm supposed to."

The bears tugged them down the airstrip to where a second helicopter sat waiting next to Shaun's.

"I suppose I'll just have to take your word for it about you two being mates. While you stink like each other, that deep metaphysical wolf shit doesn't register on us bears." Bruce handed a robe to Gem, and she took it, dressing herself quickly.

"Shaun needs clothes as well." She crossed her arms and stared at their captor.

Bruce grinned, displaying broken teeth. "I'll have to charge extra for that."

Shaun spat out blood before growling, "You can take your clothes and shove them up your—"

"Give him some clothes, or let him get some from his supply. I don't care which, but you will clothe him properly," Gem demanded. Then she turned to Shaun and slapped him on the arm. "And you, watch your tongue. I don't need to listen to that kind of talk."

Vince snickered. Norm chortled.

Bruce raised a brow. "Henpecked already, I see. You wolves need to learn how to deal with your women better. Vince, grab our guest a shirt and pants."

Shaun was hauled to the side of the chopper and offered a handful of crumpled garments. Both Vince and Norm watched closely as he pulled on the oversized clothes. Gem wrapped her robe a little tighter, stood a little straighter as she pointedly ignored the bear looming at her side. She wasn't going to give him the satisfaction of knowing exactly how scared she was.

She was pressed into the back of the helicopter, a sloppily dressed Shaun at her side, his hands tied behind him. This time when they took off there was no protective headset offered, and the noise from the propellers pounded like a hammer on an anvil in her ears. She twisted toward Shaun, pressing one ear against his chest and covering her other with her right hand.

Her left hand snuck around his back, and she clung to him, fighting the tears that threatened to fall.

"I'm so sorry. So sorry this happened." He couldn't hear her, but she needed to say it anyway. With the whining of the props overhead and Vince staring at them, it was the least likely of places for confessions, but she had to let the words out, in case she didn't get another chance. "I love you. I mean, I know our wolves like each other. Mine is very put out with me for not marking you and letting her spend time with your wolf. But it's more than that. I think you're a very special man, Shaun Stevens, and I'm glad that we're mates. And if I die in the north, that's fine, because I'll be beside you, and somehow that makes even dying okay."

She hugged him tighter and his chest moved. She wished she knew if it was because he'd heard her confession, or if she'd squeezed one of his sore spots from the beating.

With his hands tied behind him, Shaun was helpless to cradle Gem the way he wanted. The roar from the props increased the pain throbbing through his head. A shift would help him heal faster, but damn if he'd even consider that with the threat of death hanging over him. Instead he ignored his aches and nuzzled his chin against the top of her head, the only thing he could do to let her know he was there. The tear streaks on her cheeks were enough to make his wolf feral, and he wanted to do all kinds of terrible things to Curly, Larry and Mo.

The bastards flew them north and east as far as he could tell. He watched over the pilot's shoulder when he could, looking for information, hoping that wherever they did land, he could help her escape and he'd be able to steal the chopper or...

Yeah. He was hoping the crew would literally be as stupid as the Three Stooges and fall asleep or some such thing, and together he and Gem would stroll out of this without a worry.

Reality sucked.

When they landed outside one of the deserted DEW Line buildings, his whole perspective changed. This wasn't simply an impulse nab, although the fact the baddies had a chopper had kinda given that away. Unless someone knew specifically where to look, Gem could have been trapped in there forever. This was a well-executed maneuver to get cash.

The words of the big bear shifter in Chicken came back to him. Money to buy votes in the upcoming bear whoop-de-do. He and Gem had fallen victim to a money grab.

The blessed relief of the cessation of the prop noise was exchanged for increased pain as Norm shoved him in the back hard enough Shaun fell out of the chopper, face first to the ground, unable to break his fall with his hands pinned behind him.

Gem tugged him upward, brushing a hand over him gently even as she aimed the evil eye at their kidnappers. "Leave him be. There's no benefit in hurting him anymore."

"Ahh, see that one was for my brother down in Chicken. Your mate should stay out of fights that don't concern him." Norm flashed a crooked smile before shoving them toward the building.

Shaun forced himself to stay vertical and take in everything he could. If they were going to get out of this, and he had every intention of damn well making it out with both of them alive and unhurt, he needed to figure out what the hell to do.

Gem's warm hands slipped around him, helping more than he wanted to admit. Not just the physical strength, but the fact it was her, his mate. Great time to figure out that he was hopelessly in love and would do anything to make sure they stayed together.

Sections of the derelict building's siding had worked their way loose, hanging in tattered ribbons of silver and grey, the steel building posts exposed to the harsh elements. The Defense Early Warning Line buildings not actively maintained by the US and Canadian governments had been abandoned after the Cold War ended. Some had been adapted to become weather stations, some stripped by nomadic natives and shifters scavenging for building materials. This mid-sized one was in better shape than most, as they discovered after being shoved inside, the door slamming closed behind them with an ominous metallic clink. A bolt slipped into place, a lock attached.

Shaun swore. "There goes the idea of jumping them in their sleep."

A loud banging rang out—a fist pounding the door?

"You got enough supplies for a person to survive a week." Bruce's rasping laugh echoed weirdly from outside. "'Course, since there's two of you, I suggest you go on a diet or pray for mice. Once we get our money, we'll let your Daddy know where you are, sugar. And don't bother trying to figure out who we are. We'll be going bush for the next while and not even your wolves can track us. Not when we're in bear and you have no idea of our starting point."

The ear-splitting rattle resounded from the door again followed by a short silence, then the helicopter props sounded, fading slowly into the distance.

There was a ringing in Shaun's ears after the volume overload of earlier. A tomb-like hush surrounded them.

Gem clutched his shirtsleeves, her eyes wide as she stared at him. "Are they really gone?"

"It looks that way. Here, untie me."

She'd already moved to his side, and he twisted to allow her to reach his wrists. The lighting was shitty. There wasn't that much light in the sky, not even up here where the sun never set. Add to that, most of the windows seemed to be sealed with storm shutters. Only minute cracks in the siding allowed in slivers of orangish light, painting them with freaky stripes.

"This sucks. Sorry, Gem, I fucked up royally back there. I hadn't considered the idea that anyone would try to kidnap you."

She tapped his arm again. "Stop that, you're certainly not to blame. I'd forgotten about the danger myself, not realizing anyone knew who I was. It's my fault I got you into this mess."

What a ridiculous conversation. Shaun grinned, his jaw aching. "Well, now that we both got that bit of whining out of our systems... No more blame, except where it belongs—on the shits responsible."

The pressure restricting his hands vanished, and he brought his arms forward with a groan as the blood hit his fingers and flowed into the fatigued muscles.

"Are you okay?" Gem dropped the ropes to the floor and rubbed his arms gently, avoiding the rising bruises from where he'd been beaten. He'd never been so humiliated. Of course, three on one weren't good odds, but still.

"I'll be better once I shift—but first, let's take a look around. It doesn't sound as if we're in a huge rush." He stopped her before she stepped away. "I meant after I kiss you. Insane woman."

He caught her cheeks in his hands, cradling her face tenderly before lowering his lips over hers. Gem wrapped her arms around him and pressed closer. Their contact wasn't sexually frantic, but needy. Wanting. An affirmation of being together and being alive.

It was a heady kiss, and they were both breathing rather hard when they finished.

Gem slipped her fingers into his as they explored their prison. Near black surrounded them, making it tough to see where they were going. They shuffled forward, toes bumping into debris on the ground.

"At least it doesn't smell too bad."

Shaun chuckled. "That's not always a good thing. Means there isn't enough in here to attract animals, maybe not enough space to get in and out."

Gem sighed. "Call me a princess if you want, but I'm glad there's nothing dead and rotting. That would be a more than I could handle right now."

Shaun gave her shoulder a tight squeeze. "You are more than a princess, darling, but I'm with you on that one. I'm tired enough that not even my wolf is interested in a snack."

"Ewww, yuck."

Her disgusted laughter was better than the frustrated one-step-away-from-tears he'd heard in her voice the moment before. Shaun tugged her deeper into the station. "Let's find somewhere to crash. It's been a long, long day, and we might have better luck seeing what we're doing in the morning."

"You sure we shouldn't keep going tonight? Because I can, if we have to."

He peeked around the corner of a doorframe, the second one they'd come to. This time the door was intact and not hanging half off its hinges. A single cot and chair were tucked into the room.

"Ah, the penthouse suite. Here we go." He walked her forward and checked the bed for strength. "At least the asshats got that part right. It's built for shifter weight."

Gem tugged him to the bed beside her. "Are you implying I'm a heavyweight or something, Mr. Stevens?"

He leaned back without protest. He should go look around a little more, but the mattress was calling his name. "Hell no. Only this could even put up with us doing the mambo. Not that I'm saying I want to. In fact, I think for the first time in my life I will honestly say 'Not tonight, dear, I have a headache.'"

She smoothed a hand over his head, tenderly outlining one of his cuts. "Shift to your wolf. That will let us share the bed better. If you're sure about waiting until the morning."

He closed his eyes in relief. "Waiting is fine. We've been up twenty hours already. It's dark, and we're wearing sunglasses. Hit it."

There was no response.

Shaun peeled one eye open. "What? You never seen *The Blues Brothers*? I thought that was like a classic southern movie and all."

Gem shook her head, but she smiled, shifting into her wolf as she crawled beside him. He changed as well, wrapping himself around her smaller body. The steady pulse of her heartbeat slowed almost immediately, her breathing settling. He forced himself to stay awake a little longer, using his nose, his ears to examine the building as sleep rolled closer.

There was food nearby. Water. Then nothing but dust and the fading scent of bears.

Even as sleep overtook him, he realized the idiots had no idea that they were going to get the butt-whomping of their lives once he and Gem were free. One of their kidnappers was related to a bear he'd fought in Chicken? He had the contacts to take that information to the cleaners. Mess with the Takhini wolves? Mess with a Jacobs?

Hell on earth was coming down on those bear boys in very short notice. And whatever advances they'd hoped to make in their political wrangling was going to the dogs.

Or should he say wolves?

# Chapter Fourteen

Caroline dealt with another customer before responding to Evan's summons. Just because she'd become his main squeeze didn't mean he could order her around and she'd drop everything and come running.

Although in the bedroom? Holy Toledo, she'd take his orders, with an extra side to go. Sex with a wolf of Evan's caliber had turned out to be something to truly write home about. It made this façade they were pulling worthwhile on a whole new level.

She knocked on his office door, then walked in without waiting for a response, freezing when she discovered he wasn't alone.

There were two visitors. One stood against the wall, dressed in a plain dark suit. The guy could have slipped unnoticed into *The Matrix.* The other man was the center of attention. A Colonel Sanders type, with a neat mustache and beard—traces of silver showing against his dark skin. Even the spectacles were perfect—thin-rimmed, dignified. He rose to his feet, hands remaining folded on top of the head of a polished silver cane.

Caroline nodded politely.

He...sniffed, and she couldn't stop the smile that escaped. Wolves didn't seem to realize they gave themselves away in the first ten seconds of greeting anyone. That sniffing thing—it simply wasn't a human behavior. Not that she was about to say anything to *them*.

"Mr. Jacobs, this is my personal assistant, Caroline."

"She's not a wolf." The older man narrowed his gaze and examined her thoroughly. "And she smells like you. Whatever did you do to your face, girl?"

Caroline touched her still-swollen left eye involuntarily. Evan sighed as he came to her side. "Internal pack politics. It's been dealt with."

One grey brow rose skyward. "I hope the other person looks worse than you."

*Bloodthirsty wolves.* Caroline smiled, showing all her teeth. "She's in a cast, sir. My black eye is significantly less than what she's wearing."

Mr. Jacobs gave her a curt nod. "Good for you, then."

Evan tugged on Caroline's elbow. "We've got trouble, and I need your to help make some contacts."

"What's up?"

The wolf in the suit moved to stand a little closer to Mr. Jacobs as she passed him en route to the desk to grab some paper. Everything about the stiff screamed bodyguard, and if they were going for inconspicuous? Major screw-up. Not up north.

"I received a call early this morning demanding money for the return of my daughter."

Caroline frowned. "But she's with Shaun, isn't she?"

Jacobs nodded. "That's where she's supposed to be. The caller said they also had Shaun, so it's possible they were grabbed at some point after Gem's bodyguard lost them."

Caroline sat in the desk chair and glanced between Evan

and Mr. Jacobs in confusion. She and Gem had spent an entire day together, and she'd never noticed a guard. During their discussion times she'd also learned a few things about Gem's father that had pushed her hot buttons. The slight dislike factor made her less polite than she probably should have been. "There was a bodyguard? I never saw him."

"You weren't supposed to, not if he was doing his job. He was within visual range at all times, until there were a few complications." Mr. Jacobs retook his seat as Evan came to perch on the edge of her desk.

Caroline started a list of people she'd need to contact even as she listened to the conversation.

"I underestimated my girl. I didn't think she'd actually leave civilization. Once she and her guide left their second stop, the guard couldn't find a way to follow them without being noticed."

Not with them heading to the birthing grounds in northern Alaska, not unless her guard had wings. Caroline opened another screen, sending off an IM. "Evan, I can get Shaun's flight plans from the airport—there's a wolf in the traffic-control division. I assume we want to keep this on the quiet, or are we calling in the RCMP?"

The wolf-in-a-suit and Mr. Jacobs exchanged confused glances.

"Royal Canadian Mounted Police—the local authorities. If Gem's been kidnapped—"

Jacobs frowned. "No police. It's a shifter situation. I want it dealt with quietly if possible. We'll go to the humans as a last resort."

About what she figured. It had to be some shifter-ego-mojo thing, but they never seemed to want to use the proper system. "Then may I ask what kind of manpower you can provide?"

"To assist in recovering them?"

Caroline nodded. "If we're not contacting the police, I want to know we're not going into this blind and getting them both killed, not if they have actually been kidnapped. Shaun's a good friend, and I enjoyed Gem's company while she was here."

Mr. Jacobs narrowed his gaze, the sweet old man disappearing and the predator of his wolf showing through. "You think I would do anything to harm my daughter?"

"Caroline…" Evan's tone warned her off, then he shrugged and that damn grin of his was back in place. In other words, he mustn't have thought she was in too deep of shit, but she was going to have to talk her way out of this one alone.

*Bastard.* Another test? She was so going to mix something nasty into his coffee tomorrow morning.

Caroline straightened her spine and maintained eye contact with Mr. Jacobs even though she wanted to duck behind Evan and hide. "Respectfully, I think you aren't from around here, sir. This isn't the civilized south, and we're not talking about hopping on a bus or in a cab to get to wherever they are. It's not about money, although our pack resources aren't unlimited. If you've got help available—that changes our game plan."

Jacobs relaxed back, his eyes bright. Feral. "You find out where they are, young lady. I have the wolves, and the funds, to get the damn fools who snatched my girl and make them sorry they ever started anything with me and my kin. You'll find we're not all that civilized when it comes to people threatening our families."

They stared at each other for a moment, and Caroline relented. She'd dealt with enough wolves over the years to know when one was bullshitting her. The old man really was trying to provide what he thought was best for Gem.

"Let me make a few calls." Caroline tilted her chin at Evan. "I've got a list for you as well. You'll have to speak to the Alpha in Dawson—he won't talk to me."

Evan nodded, and the two of them got to work.

Gem woke to see dust motes floating past in horizontal lines, the sun shining in through the tiny slits in the windows enough to show her that she was alone in bed. There was a warm spot where Shaun had lain by her side all night.

Maybe falling asleep last night had been a bad idea, but she'd been one step away from falling over. Not much dignity in that. Although maintaining her dignity was the least of her worries at the moment.

She hopped off the cot, stretching and shaking her fur into place before following Shaun's scent into the back of the building.

"Well, good morning, sleeping beauty." He knelt and caressed her, scratching behind one ear, and Gem snorted at him. Wolves were allowed to snort, right?

He looked much better than he had yesterday, the bruises fading, the cut above his eye sealed over and healing already. She butted him with her head, wishing for the millionth time they could speak to each other like a regular mated pair, sharing thoughts mentally.

"I've been examining our home. It's actually quite lovely, and I think I spotted a mistake our kidnappers made. If you wouldn't mind staying in wolf for a moment?"

She shook her head and followed as he guided her to another section. The corridor led inward, away from the exterior walls. The building was large enough there were no windows in this section.

"I think someone had adapted this DEW Line for science

experiments before it was abandoned. The bears who stuffed us in here must be Alaskan or Northern Yukon born. They did an awesome job making sure your average wolf would be stuck like a fish in a barrel."

Shaun tugged open a half-size door and squatted, pointing into a small square opening.

Gem sat on her haunches. Oh fudge, she bet she knew where this was going. He'd called her insane before. It was his turn for the label if he thought she'd go along with this without some sweet-talking.

She was going to make him say it, because volunteering to crawl into a black, spider-web-filled metal box when she didn't know where it went?

"I can't fit. A bear damn well can't fit, but you can. This is part of the heating system. The central furnace—they simply ran the ducting along the floors. We only need to get to the other side of this wall, and from what I saw as we were entering, there's a good chance there's a break in the exterior and you can get outside. Once you're free, we'll work on how you can spring me."

Gem nodded, then ignored him and paced back to the "bedroom". The duct was a great idea. An awesome idea. She had no issues with any of it.

But first she was going to have breakfast, just to get up her nerve.

She jumped on the bed and shifted before reaching up for a hug. Shaun tugged her against him, his hands nice and warm as they stroked her bare back. "I thought you were going to crawl through the ducting right away."

She squeezed him hard, then looked around for her robe. It was crumpled and dirty, and she couldn't be happier to have something to tug on to give her the illusion of protection, at least for a little longer. "No, you suggested I go right away. I want something to eat, please, and maybe a washroom?"

Shaun kissed her nose. "I'm sorry. I was so excited when I started looking around that I didn't even think—"

She stuck her palm over his mouth. "You know what? You don't have to do it all—have all the answers, solve all the puzzles. Work with me, just like you taught me on the trail. Right?"

Shaun caught her wrist in his fingers, nibbling on her fingertips for a moment. "My apologies. You're right. I'm used to being the one in charge—excursions, and all that. But since this is my first kidnapping, I should totally follow your lead— *oof.*"

Gem shook out the knuckles of her left hand. "You have wonderful abdomen muscles."

"If you want to examine them, feel free to use your tongue, not your fist." Shaun pointed behind her. "They left a cooler with food in it. Shall I make you a sandwich while you use the little girl's room? It's around the corner to the left. A lovely plastic bucket complete with TP and a squirt bottle of sanitizer."

She stood for a moment until her sense of the ridiculous hit hard. She'd run for miles in wolf form, made love on the side of a mountain. Sat by a fire under the midnight sun.

This was simply another part of the adventure, wasn't it?

"A sandwich would be lovely. Is there anything to drink?"

Shaun winked at her. "You're not going to believe this, but there are bottles of Perrier."

*Gag.* "Really?"

She slipped away to examine the facilities. If they were too freaky she'd shift back to wolf and pee in the corner.

His voice carried to her. "Yeah, I guess one of them figured you being a genteel lady and such, you needed the good stuff."

"Do they know Perrier tastes horrible? And smells like stinky socks."

A loud guffaw rang out. "No shit?"

A terrible temptation overwhelmed her. "That's right. Shit is a perfect description."

She stepped back into the bedroom in time to see his jaw fall open. "Gemmita Ellen Louise May Jacobs, did my ears deceive me or did you just use the word shit?"

Laughter bubbled up, urged on by the expression on his face.

"Poop? Crap? How did you put it once? Bloody fucking—"

This time his hand slapped across her mouth. "Who are you, and what have you done to my Gem?"

She smiled and he released her. "I do know the big bad words, Shaun, I choose not to use them. But I think in light of our circumstances, there's a few choice swears that need to be aired."

"As long as your father doesn't think I corrupted you or something."

*Her father.* "Oh boy, I bet he's not happy right now."

Shaun handed her a sandwich as she sat on the lone chair. "You get kidnapped often? Just so I can make plans and such."

The ham and cheese was delicious after having had nothing but rabbit for the past however many hours. "First time. Maybe that's part of the reason I was kept protected. It's a bit of a problem of my own making, leaving the easy-to-protect zone."

Shaun finished his first sandwich and dug into another. "Love, if people want to grab you, they're going to try if you're walking the streets of Whitehorse or hidden away in a cloister. It might be tougher for them to succeed in the second case, but that's not a great way to live, now, is it?"

Gem chewed thoughtfully. He was right. She was enjoying being out and about in the "real world". She watched him as he watched her. There was something there, more than the mate bond. For a moment she considered repeating her words from the plane, making sure he heard her this time, but this wasn't the setting for confessions of love and forever.

She'd been frightened back before they started the return trip to the chopper. Scared by how much she'd come to care for him, and how close she'd come to giving over control to him. Allowing him to make the decision of where they would live, and what they would do.

There had to be the balance, between them being a partnership and being individuals with ideas of their own. It wasn't about getting what she wanted anymore, but making sure that she didn't give up on herself in the midst of becoming one with him.

None of that seemed the thing to share while they were locked in a prison.

But once they were free? Look out.

"Gaag."

Gem glanced up to see Shaun's face contorted into the most awful grimace. "Are you okay?"

He pointed at his mouth and wrinkled his nose. In his hand he clutched one of the distinctive green bottles and she giggled. He swallowed hard, the exaggerated movement making her laugh even harder.

"I warned you!"

"Actually, I've tasted worse." Shaun winked at her before taking another swig, his expression thoughtful. He shook his head. "Nah, I'll take a double shot of Sourdough Toe any day."

*Sourdough Toe?* She patted her mouth against her sleeve and stripped off the robe. "I guess it's time to pretend I'm a mole instead of a wolf."

His gaze followed her as she stood. She bent to drop a kiss on his cheek then walked out the door back toward the open vent. If she happened to let her hips wiggle extra hard, it was his own fault.

"Tease."

"Uh-huh." Gem darted a glance over her shoulder to see him following along, eating her hungrily with his gaze. "I hope *you* don't have to crawl any time soon, because you're not going to be able to get that weapon to remain concealed."

He grinned at her. "Kidnapping has done wonders for your sense of humour."

Gem had to agree. "I think it's the whole northern air. I must be allergic."

She shifted, paws slipping out of her outsized shoes. Shaun moved the door aside farther, and she stuck her nose in as far as she could without actually putting her head into the duct.

"I did brush it out with a stick earlier," Shaun boasted.

*Her hero.*

Gem dropped to her elbows and crawled forward an inch at a time, following the fresh air coming from in front of her. Crawling was slow going, the duct squeezed tighter in places where there must have been outside damage to the casing.

Oh God, she'd better not get stuck. She wasn't claustrophobic, but it would be almost impossible to get out without help.

"You still moving?" Shaun called, his voice echoing strangely in the tight metal quarters.

She yipped confirmation. Crawled another couple inches.

Sneezed.

"Bless you."

She really shouldn't laugh—it was tough enough already to breathe in the dark with four sides closing in around her. But common everyday politenesses like a gesundheit?

She must be getting giddy. Or steps away from hysterical.

The panel on her right wiggled, and her hopes leapt. She leaned to the side harder, and a gust of fresh air hit her in the face. She howled, and from a distance Shaun's voice rumbled back with delight.

"You there?"

Not yet, but close. She snuck forward a little more, pushed hard with her nose, and with a crash, the flap beside her fell away and she rolled free.

She shifted and clapped her hands in delight. "I'm out. I did it. Shaun, I did it!"

Even as he crowed back at her, praising her loudly, Gem examined the new room she'd discovered. There was no door on the outside wall, but the window let in a ton of light—more of the storm shutter was broken away in this section.

"Can you see a way to outside?" Shaun asked.

"Maybe. Give me a minute."

She picked a careful path over the dirt-strewn floor, cold rocks and stray bits of garbage poking into her less-than-wolf-proof arches. But what she discovered more than made up for the aches and pains.

"There's a fresh breeze blowing in. The window is broken, Shaun, and I'm sure I'll be able to get out."

"Awesome. Take your time. Don't rush. Use whatever you need that helps."

Gem stopped. While she wanted to race forward and try the

shutters, there was too much broken glass to go anywhere fast. She needed some thing to step on, or a broom. There was a desk in the corner, with a chair leaning against the frame. From the dust on the floor showing her steps, the kidnappers had never even entered this section of the building. Boxes of electronic equipment lay piled in heaps beside one wall, along with a discarded lab coat and rubber boots.

Saks Fifth Avenue, it wasn't, but as if she was going to complain.

As she slipped on the coat, one of the objects piled in the chaos caught her eye. "Shaun, can you hear me?"

"What's up? You find a way out?"

"Haven't checked closer yet," she confessed. "I was putting on some clothes I found. I think there's something in here you need to see."

"Cryptic."

She laughed as she tipped the boots over and crashed them together to remove any spiders or little critters making their home inside. Peering in didn't help, so she gathered her courage and slipped a hand in. Slowly. Very slowly.

When all she hit was sole, the sense of relief was powerful.

Of course, she wasn't as lucky in the second boot.

Her scream died away in time for guilt to descend as she heard Shaun's frantic yells.

"Gem. What the fuck is wrong?"

"It's okay. I'm okay." Her skin crawled as she pulled out a dead mouse from where it had been jammed into the toe of the boot. "I was having a girly moment. Sorry for scaring you."

The banging died down, and even through the walls his sigh was audible. "Princess moment, eh? Is something dead?"

*Poop.* "You know me too well."

"Not nearly as well as I plan to. So what's the thing I need to see? And I'm not trying to rush you, but I'm getting hoarse from yelling. Is outside a possibility?"

"Nag, nag, nag." Gem grabbed the curly cord she'd spotted poking from the box and gave a light tug. A microphone pulled free, followed by the corner of a boxlike object. She shoved aside the rest of the pile and rescued her find.

With her treasure under her arm, she made her way to the window.

"Good news, I can do this. Give me two more minutes."

Shaun chuckled. "It's not like I'm going anywhere…"

Gem wiggled boxes closer, making a platform under the window. As she hauled one away from the wall, she spotted a fire extinguisher and fire axe, nabbing the latter happily. "Okay, I'm making some noise. Don't worry, it's demolition time."

"Have fun!"

There was something freeing about swinging the axe, forcing the few remaining struts on the one side to bend enough she could reach the outer layer. After spreading what was left of a rotting blanket over the glass shards, she shoved the far-left section of the storm shutters away, the loud screech of metal on metal ringing through the room.

The bright morning sunshine matched her mood as she dropped both her discovery and the axe to the outside ground, crawled up on the window ledge, and wiggled her way out.

Intense satisfaction sparkled like tiny bubbles inside. She didn't want to shout, she was too full of pride and happiness. Instead, she grabbed her supplies and walked cautiously around the perimeter of the building. On the off-chance there was someone hiding in the area, she wasn't going to walk into another trap.

Nothing but fresh air, the gentle noises of the tundra, and after her second corner, the front door with a deadbolt lock hanging from it.

She emptied her hands and knocked.

Shaun's soft response came from just on the other side of the door. "I knew you'd do it."

That he was already there, waiting for her, was huge. The impulse to burst out with a confession of love was so strong—but she still wanted to wait. "Thank you. Now, I need to get you out. Let me try this. Careful, it could get noisy."

She swung at the lock, the first couple blows going off-angle and accomplishing not much more than making her ears ring. Then she turned the axe around, using the blunt backside of the head, and the metal twisted.

"It's working, Shaun."

"Woohoo, break me outta here, love."

Another half-dozen blows were all it took. The lock fell into two pieces with a satisfying crash. She opened the bolt and drew it back. The door swung open, and she found herself lifted high into the air, spun in circles as Shaun squeezed her tight.

Then his lips were on hers and they were kissing. Mouths locked together, tongues tangling. She clutched his broad shoulders and smiled against him.

They drew apart, both grinning like fools.

"Well, so much for being trapped." Shaun examined her carefully, his fingers skimming over her. "You okay? Nothing happen when you screamed? No cuts, no..."

"I'm fine. But thank you for asking."

She cuddled to his side as he twisted to take in their surroundings. "Well, at least I don't have to worry about getting shot or beat on again. Man, they did abandon us."

"Probably figured I'd be trapped and why bother to stick around." Indignation rose. "I wish I could give them a piece of my mind. If they'd been wolves..."

Shaun hugged her again. "I'm pretty sure that's why they were bears. You and I together can do a lot of damage to another pair of wolves, just by how strong we are. But all the hierarchy power in the world doesn't work against different breeds of shifter."

Under her ear, his heart pulsed with steady beat. "I'm ready to go home."

He lifted her chin, smiling even as he shared the bad news. "Sorry, but that's going to take a bit of work. The markings on the station give me a rough idea of where we are. I know from my days plotting trips up to Old Crow we've got a ways to hoof it. Still, in wolf we can do it. You okay with that?"

Gem batted her lashes at him. "You don't want to call for a ride?"

Shaun raised a brow, and she snuck out from under his arm, grabbed her discovery and held it out to him. "Of course, I'm not positive this works, but I'm pretty sure I saw a flashlight in the prison room, that will have batteries. Plus, there were a lot of other wires and things in the room I broke out of. I figured a smart guy like you would totally be able to make this work."

Shaun accepted the box from her, delight on his face. "You found a bloody ham radio."

"Is that what this is?"

He nodded. "Damn, you scored big. Come on, I think we should order in room service with this thing. You want anchovies on the pizza?"

They moved back into the station. Gem buzzed with excitement to have been able to play a vital role in saving not only herself, but him. They worked together well as a team. And

225

as he pulled apart the flashlight and twisted wires, Gem watched her mate, content to be at his side.

# Chapter Fifteen

Waiting for the rescue team to reach them took less time than Shaun expected. Then again, he should have been suspicious when he used the ham radio and discovered word of their kidnapping was already common knowledge, at least in the wolf-shifter world.

When the first person out of the chopper was Caroline, Shaun wasn't surprised. She was Evan's assistant after all. But the tall, slender man who crawled out after her made his fur stand on end.

Gem squealed. She raced forward and threw herself at the man Shaun assumed was her father. Oh boy. On a scale of one to ten, running away was looking like a twenty-seven. The stern look the dude tossed his direction was pretty damn clear in showing what the old man thought of his baby girl's choice of companions.

Good thing Gem's mate selection wasn't up to her father. Shaun smiled broadly.

Caroline made her way to his side. The most extraordinary colours decorated her face. "What the hell happened to you?" he asked.

She tossed him a grin. "You seen *your* face in a mirror lately?"

Oh, right. "There were three of them. They caught me from

behind. They used laser beams and rancid pudding."

"You forget to duck?"

He couldn't get over her bruises. "I'm serious, Caroline. Has the world gone mad?" He sniffed. "Holy shit, you've been fucking around with Evan."

She was laughing too hard to be offended. "No, the world isn't mad. Or no madder than usual. Yes, Evan and I are seeing each other. Get over it. I'm here to escort Mr. Jacobs 'to the rescue' since he refused to remain behind. Evan is already working on getting a bead on the guys who jumped you—thanks for the note to start looking in Chicken. The bear shifters we talked to in Dawson were outraged that any of them would stoop to kidnapping—we have their full co-operation as well. Anyone laying a hand on Gem in the future will be given clan discipline, which I hear is actually tougher than what wolves hand out. Go figure."

Shaun blinked hard. "Can you repeat that last part?"

She frowned. "Which part?"

"I kinda got stuck when you said you and Evan are seeing each other. What the fuck is he thinking?"

He didn't see the blow coming, and by some freaky circumstance, she slammed him right on the most tender section of his ribs, and he folded like a card table. The ground hadn't gotten any softer since the last time he smacked into it. He rolled to stare up at her, the bright sky haloed around her pretty blonde head.

"Dude. I speak wolf." Her sweet smile belied the steel in her tone. "You know the rules. I'm with Evan. Next time you bitch at me, I kick you in the nuts. I would imagine you'd like to keep them intact, having found your mate and all."

He accepted her outstretched hand and crawled to his feet. "Yup, got it. Congrats, etc. etc. Good to know. The chicks hanging all over him were driving the old guy a little insane."

She muttered something that sounded like "you're telling me" as she gestured him forward to where Gem stood speaking with her father.

The props on the chopper turned slowly, the sound barely disturbing the air. It was quiet enough that the lecture Mr. Jacobs delivered carried on the breeze far too easily. Gem waited in front of him, hands tucked in front of her, the rest of her body rigid and erect as if she wore a corset and had a book balanced on her head.

Shaun cleared his throat. Their gazes swung his direction. He wiggled his fingers. "Ho."

Gem bit her lip, fighting back a smile.

Shaun stepped forward, hand held out to her dad. Only one way through and that was full-speed ahead. "Mr. Jacobs. Great to finally meet you. Thanks for coming to escort us home."

"And you are...?" The long, slow perusal up and down was followed by sudden comprehension. "Oh yes, the guide. Good to meet you as well."

Then he turned his back and attempted to steer Gem toward the chopper.

Shaun tapped him on the shoulder. "Sir?"

Mr. Jacobs paused. "What? Oh...of course." He dug into his pocket and pulled out a wallet, grabbed a couple bills and pressed them into Shaun's hand. "Here you go."

Shaun closed his hand around the man's fingers. "Sir. No. You need to listen for a minute."

"Shaun, allow me." Gem's sweet voice snuck into his ears and tickled him into submission. He let go and raised his hands in surrender. If she wanted to do this, he'd let her.

Then she slipped under his arm and cuddled in close, and

Mr. Jacobs' jaw dropped.

"Daddy, I'd like you to meet Shaun Stevens. Yes, he's my guide, but he's also my mate."

Wind swept over the North Pole and rattled in his future father-in-law's open mouth. "Mate?"

She nodded.

Jacobs raised his head and narrowed his eyes. "Is this some kind of post-traumatic induced psychoses? Because I would understand—"

"Use your nose, dude," Shaun blurted out. *Oops.* Forgot the polite bit. "Sir."

There was no denying the dismay on the old man's face this time. "Well, damn."

"Daddy!" Gem stood to one side.

"Well, darling, it's a little unexpected. Why didn't you tell me?" He peered at them. "You aren't marked. Why aren't you marked if you're mates?"

She wrinkled her nose and shifted uneasily on her feet. "It's...complicated."

Shaun snorted—he simply couldn't stop it. Complicated? That was one way to describe their relationship.

Caroline stepped forward. "If I could make a suggestion, we should move this to the chopper. We need to get back to Dawson and the rest of the search crew."

Gem shook her head. "I don't want to go back to Dawson."

*She didn't?* Shaun waited with bated breath to see what was next on the agenda.

Gem faced her father. "Thank you for coming and getting us." She turned to include Caroline in the conversation. "We really appreciate it. And I do hope there's a group going after the kidnappers. But what Shaun and I need is a ride back to his helicopter, or better yet to somewhere close to our abandoned campsite."

Caroline nodded slowly. "I believe we can arrange that. I'll have to double-check with the pilot."

She took off toward the helicopter.

"What you doing, love?" Shaun smoothed a hand down her back and she melted against him. She was perfect there, and it was so right to hold her in his arms. There was another option—and while it wasn't what he wanted, he had to offer her the choice. "I can go get the chopper if you want to go back to Dawson with your father."

"I think that's for the best," Jacobs interjected. "We can meet in Whitehorse and discuss the rest of—"

"No." Gem stared at her father. "Did you not hear what I just said?"

"Darling, you've had a traumatic experience."

"Darn tootin', I have."

Shaun fought to hide his grin as her father's eyes widened. "Gem!"

"Daddy, Shaun and I need to go back. We have to retrieve the equipment we abandoned. I have my research notes to gather. If you'd like to wait for us in Whitehorse, you're welcome to—Evan Stone seems to be a very accommodating Alpha. But I, and my mate, have some other business to attend to first. I hope you understand."

Shaun was so proud he wanted to howl. Instead, he kept rubbing her back, letting her know he was there if she needed him.

Mr. Jacobs folded his arms across his chest. "I see. That's the way it's going to be, is it?"

Gem nodded curtly, then softened. "Thank you for coming.

I love you, Daddy."

How could any male resist when she pulled that sweet, innocent face on him?

"I love you too, pumpkin." Jacobs stared at Shaun for a moment. "You. We'll be having a long talk the next time we meet, young man."

Shaun resisted temptation. Oh, the things he could say right now. "Looking forward to it, sir."

Crossing the short distance to the helicopter and finding places for everyone was bizarre in its normality. Anticlimactic even, like they were out for a sightseeing tour.

The chopper was full and noisy, jammed in with the pilot, this weird dude in a suit, Gem's father, Caroline and him and Gem. But the way his mate curled against his body, and settled his hand over her warm belly made the discomfort of being squeezed into one seat more than tolerable.

If he could just figure out what the hell was going on.

He really could nab the chopper on his own. She could spend some time with her father, have a hot bath and return to civilization. Of course, the chances of her deciding to stay with him in the north grew dimmer by the minute.

Their entire relationship had been a comedy of errors, and it was only by sheer chance that the kidnapping hadn't turned out any more violent and bloody. The north hadn't shown itself in the best light.

Gem, however, had shone like a diamond. It was clear his fragile princess had a rock-solid core, and a lot more inside her head than he'd given her credit for at the start. And a lot more than her father understood.

They were dropped off an appropriate distance from the tent. Caroline tapped him on the shoulder as Gem said her goodbyes to her father.

"I can make sure he stays distracted for a while, or send him home. Which do you prefer?"

Shaun sighed. He knew what he wanted, but Gem hadn't said a word. If she decided to return south, she should travel with her father. Safety in numbers and all that. "Distract him. We'll only be four, five days, at the most. The herd should be gone by then, and we'll grab our stuff and return."

She nodded. "For what it's worth, I hope she stays."

"Me too." Very, *very* much.

Gem ran, working her shorter legs hard to keep up with Shaun. She liked that he didn't slow down for her anymore, that he pushed on and found a comfortable tempo to run. She was able to maintain the pace better now than when she'd started this adventure.

That's what she needed to let him know. While seeing her father had brought up some doubts and concerns, it had also made one truth that much clearer. She and Shaun belonged together. Figuring out where to live was the least of their worries.

If her daddy had any idea of taking her back south against her will? There would be none of that. Plus, the one detail she and Shaun needed to complete? It was going to happen soon.

Her wolf shivered with anticipation.

They slowed as they reached the outskirts of their campsite, her heart pounding from the exertion and from the thrill of her secret plans. She tossed back her head and breathed deeply. The caribou were still in the area, their scent strong in her nostrils, but not as strong as she anticipated.

Ahead of her, Shaun had shifted back to human. She joined him, checking the landscape from their lookout perch.

He pointed to the side. "There. The caribou have already changed location. Not much, but enough we can get at our things."

She squeezed him briefly before they shifted and returned to the tent.

They made quick work of packing, silent for the most part, talking as they gathered the scattered objects. Even a single night later, the animals and winds had begun to take their human possessions back to the wild. Gem smiled as she examined the chewed toe of a sock, the fabric shredded to fuzz, some no doubt stolen away for a nest or a burrow. She carefully pulled the rest of the sock apart and deposited the scraps into the scoop of a hollow at the edge of a bush. One of the small creatures of the tundra would find the supplies soon enough.

Pulling her hiking boots back on was painful, yet not as bad as she expected. The happiness she experienced every time they bumped elbows or rocked into each other in the tent...there was no containing how much she truly enjoyed being with him now.

They hit the path, and once they'd walked far enough their voices wouldn't disturb anything, conversation began again.

"I'm sorry if I blew it with your father."

Gem laughed. "He should be apologizing to you. And to me. That wasn't what I expect of him."

"Really?"

*Well...* "Okay, yes, he's very decisive about what he wants for me, but I didn't think he'd question if we really were mates."

Shaun fell silent. She understood his reticence. There wasn't much he could say. While neither of them had ever denied their mating, they hadn't been shouting it out to the world either, had they? She hadn't marked him, she hadn't confirmed they would stay together.

A string of swear words bubbled inside, wanting very badly to escape. Northern air getting to her again, or simply what really needed to be said.

Gem paced closer to Shaun, to make sure he heard her question. "We going to camp one night on the way back?"

"I think so. You good to hike for a little longer tomorrow?"

Definitely, since she had plans for tonight. "That's fine."

They fell silent, the rhythm of hiking smooth and almost hypnotic as his feet hit the path ahead of her again and again. Thoughts raced through her mind in an endless loop.

*North, south, north, south.*

She had no idea, no way to know which was better. The only thing she knew for certain was that she had to be by his side.

They set up the tent again, got a pot of water going. Shaun sat across from her as she leaned away from lighting the stove, the most peculiar expression on his face.

"What?"

"You look... No, it's silly."

Gem knelt back and planted her fists on her hips. "What?"

"You look good."

Lot of work for a little compliment, but she'd take it. "Thank you."

He didn't stop staring. And she couldn't stop staring back. Her wolf bumped her, hard. Really hard, and she swallowed with need.

Screw supper, she wanted her mate.

She turned off the burner and his brow rose. When she stood and reached down a hand to him, he smiled. "Are we fasting?"

"Shut up."

"Shutting."

The tent was small and cozy after the cold metal of the DEW Line building, the light making the blue nylon fabric glow above their heads. She scrambled out of her clothes, reaching to find he'd already joined her.

They tumbled together onto the sleeping-bag-covered Therm-a-Rests.

"Shaun?"

What to say? Or should she simply do? The questions disappeared when he rolled her to her back and lowered his head to kiss and suck on her breasts. He held her, cupping and supporting her as he drew the tips into his mouth and made her crazy.

There was a physical addiction happening here, and Gem had no intention of attempting to find a cure.

She scratched her nails down his body, pulling a groan of happiness from his lips. As she sat upright, he wiggled away, until with very little effort she had hold of the base of his cock, a trembling note of approval breaking free.

"What are you doing to me, love?"

Gem licked the salty seed from the slit, wetting the heated head of his shaft with her tongue before pulling away to respond. "If you have to ask, I must be doing it wrong."

"No, no, totally right. Totally, oh my fucking—"

She'd enveloped his length completely, taking as much as possible, as deep as possible. The continued happy noises escaping him pleased her. Made the tingling and aching between her legs increase as well, wetness brushing her thighs. But she didn't want to rush this. It had been a long time coming, and she was going to do everything right.

Slow drag up, quicker plunge down. She wrapped her fingers around the base of his erection, letting herself descend that far on each bob, her saliva coating him and easing the way. When she pressed her tongue hard along the underside of his shaft, he jerked his hips, catching hold of her head and freezing her in position.

"Don't...move."

Gem pulsed her lips and sucked.

"Arghhh, don't do that either." A series of short pants burst from him as he pulled himself free, lifting her from his groin.

She turned her most innocent face his direction. "But I wasn't finished."

He blew out a slow stream of air through pursed lips as he tweaked her nose. "We were nearly done before we began."

"I wanted you to come."

He grinned. "Oh, I will. But ladies first."

Okay. She could work with that.

Somehow he flipped them around, and instead of her on top, giving to him, it was all about what he could do to drive her crazy.

He teased her nipples with his fingers. Trailed kisses down her belly, and licked the inside of her thighs. When she giggled, he planted his palms on her legs and pressed them apart, staring down at her sex with craving in his eyes.

And then...the things he did with his tongue were indescribable. Her mind went foggy right about the time he slipped a finger into her core. The first orgasm went off and she sighed.

He didn't stop. A second finger joined the first, pressure building rapidly without a break as he licked and sucked, tossing her over another peak, and another, until she lay quivering with the excessive pleasure driving through her veins.

She pulled together enough strength to force herself vertical, crawled into his lap and with one sure motion, joined them.

They both clung tight, as if afraid the other would disappear. Vanish like a dream upon waking. Gem didn't want this to end. She belonged with Shaun, and if she admitted the truth to herself, the idea of living in the north didn't scare her anymore. Not like it had at first.

Because she'd have him.

She rose and fell over him, a constant, rhythmic dance that increased in tempo and pressure until she pounded down, his hips canting upward to greet her on each movement. Her fingers tangled in his hair, tugging him closer, and she took a deep breath, her nose buried right beside his ear.

Her wolf howled with delight as she opened her mouth and caught hold of his shoulder muscle between her teeth.

Shaun froze, his cock sunk to the root in her core. "Gem?"

She closed her lips, added a slight pressure. Asking permission without saying a word.

"Oh hell, love, yeah. Bite me."

He grabbed the back of her head with one hand and pressed her harder to his shoulder. At the same time he drove his hips upward like a mad man, his erection pistoning in and out, thrusting her over into a climax just as she bit down. Marking him. Making him hers.

He threw back his head and damn near screamed. Gem laughed, her orgasm pulsing on and on, then igniting into something out of this world as he yanked her closer. He fastened his mouth on her neck, and a second later, stars were all she saw as his teeth pressed into her flesh.

*"I love you."*

Sweet mercy. She'd heard him. In her head, just like that first time they'd made love.

*"Shaun?"*

She wanted to try again, wanted to see if it was real, but the pleasure streaking through her couldn't be denied, not even to experiment with their potential mate connection. She held on tight and rode out the storm.

When she could think again, it was to discover him stroking her back, fingertips gentle along her ribs, dipping down her waist before cupping her butt then rising up in endless circles.

*"I've waited my entire life to experience this."*

Shaun kissed her temple. *"I have to agree."*

Tears rushed into her eyes. *"It's real then? You can hear me?"*

He nuzzled her neck, licking where he'd marked her, and a shiver shook her against him, rubbing their skin together. *"You're in my soul, love. Hearing you this way is just the icing on the cake."*

# Chapter Sixteen

Shaun stared across the Moonshine Pub at Gem, wondering how it was possible for them to be so connected, and him still have no bloody idea was going on in that pretty head of hers.

Odds were he was simply too stupid to read the signs.

A couple of women from the pack wandered over and joined the table, leaning in to chat with Gem and Caroline. The four ladies laughed freely, their heads close together. To their left, Gem's father sipped from a large brandy glass, a group of old-timers gathered at his side shooting the breeze and trying to one up each other with fish stories. The stiff in the suit leaned on the wall, a dark pair of glasses covering his eyes.

Shaun shook his head and turned his gaze back to his mate. She was far more interesting to look at, even if the secretive glances being tossed his direction from the four women made him nervous.

"You going to tell me what's got you looking so constipated?" Evan slammed a new beer on the table in front of him, then propped himself up on the tall stool to Shaun's right.

Shaun took a constitutional swig of the brew before pointing the mouth of his bottle in the direction of the ladies. "I don't understand what you're doing with a human who's not your mate, but hell if I'm going to give you shit when I've got a mate and don't quite know what I'm doing either."

Evan lifted his drink and saluted him. "Women. Can't live with them, can't find the car keys without them."

They set down their bottles at the same time, simultaneous sighs escaping as they stared at the women.

Shaun shot a glance at Evan.

Evan snorted.

Then the laughter set in for real, and they were lost. Shaun had tears streaming down his face right about the time Evan fell off his stool. Things kinda went downhill from there.

Every time Shaun managed to catch his breath, Evan started up again and set him off. Shaun clutched his stomach, the pain almost as bad as being beaten black and blue. Somehow they were both on the floor, dragging themselves up against the wall and hoping for a reprieve.

*"Do I need to come and rescue you?"*

The sweet touch of Gem's voice in his mind hadn't grown old. Not as they had traveled from the camp to the chopper, not over the past couple days as they'd shown her father around Whitehorse.

It calmed him and excited him all in the same breath. She was in his core, and he couldn't imagine living without her.

*"Nah, we're okay. You having fun with the girls?"* He tried poking his head around the barstool legs to spot her face again.

*"Yes, but what I'd like is..."*

When she stopped, a touch of longing in her tone, it was enough to sober him up from his giggle fest. He groaned as he slapped Evan on the shoulder, his stomach protesting as he sat up. "On that note, I'll be back. My mate needs something, and your ugly mug just don't cut it anymore."

Evan waved him off as they both rolled to their knees.

*"Now you should know better than to stop in the middle of that kind of a sentence. Me being the hound dog I am, I could find all kinds of fascinating ways to finish that thought."*

She watched as he approached, her dark lashes fluttering over her bright eyes. Her mouth curved in a smile meant all for him. *"That sounds more interesting than what I was going to ask."*

Shaun stopped at her side, nodding politely at the rest of the table. "Ladies. If you don't mind, I'd like to borrow Gem for a few minutes."

For a bunch of grown wolves, there was far too much winking and nodding happening as she took his hand. Shaun's face grew hot at the blunt stares from Caroline and the other girls. What the hell had they been talking about, and holy shit, was he actually blushing?

This night got weirder by the minute.

Gem squeezed his fingers. "Where we going?"

Shaun tugged her close, his hand slipping to her lower back to keep them close. "Dance floor for now."

They swayed easily, the music nice and slow. Gem draped her arms around his neck, the move lifting her breasts against him.

*Hmmm.*

They danced, bodies comfortable, in harmony. Part of what he'd longed for was right there. Complete connection, total belonging. There was no question about that truth—he and Gem were together.

"Shaun, we need to make some decisions."

He turned her slowly, holding on to the peace for one more moment. "There was only one decision that had to be made, love, and you already made it when you marked me."

Gem stiffened. "When...I marked you?"

Shaun nodded, attempting to guide her from the dance floor toward the open patio. "Come here, let's not do this in the middle of the entire pack."

She resisted. "No, this is as fine a place as any."

Somehow she twisted from his arms and took a spot a few feet from him. He missed her warmth immediately, and the sadness in her eyes haunted him. "Gem, what's wrong?"

"Just because I marked you, and you marked me doesn't mean you get to make all the decisions. I thought you understood that. I thought that was clear when we worked together, on the trail, when we escaped from being kidnapped."

Complete confusion swirled around him. "Gem? You lost me. I just meant that—I mean, all I wanted to say, is that I love you."

"I love you too, but..." She sighed, an aching, lonely sound, enough to break his heart.

Shaun scratched his head. "There seem to be whole gaps missing from this conversation. I'm not making any decisions. I'm telling you I'm willing to move south. Check it out for a while. Shit, maybe I'll learn how to windsurf in your ocean. And I'll take ballroom-dance lessons, or whatever the hell else you do for fun down south."

Gem stared at him.

The entire bar seemed to hold their breath. The music faded, the *flap flap flap* of the overhead fans loud in his ears.

She tilted her head to the side. "You...want to move south?"

Shaun caught her hands in his. "I want to be with you, wherever you want to be. If that's back in Georgia, I'm not that old a dog. I can learn new tricks."

She swallowed hard, her lower lip trembling. "You mean

it?"

He nodded. *"Of all the things in life I'm willing to give up, you're not one of them. I need you, Gem."*

Gem threw her arms around his neck and squeezed him tight. "I don't know what to say. Really? You would give up your life here to be with me...?"

Her voice tightened, the words dying away.

He kissed her cheek gently. "Really. Why is that so hard to believe?"

*"Because you love the north."*

Moving wouldn't be easy, but it would work. He'd make it work.

*"I love you more,"* he vowed.

She melted, her expression of complete adoration making his heart pound.

"I need time to settle details with Tad, and the business end of things. But other than that, I'm good."

"That's a fine young man you've got there." Mr. Jacobs' voice interrupted them, the swirl of others discussing his confession filling the air.

Gem turned to face her father, tucking herself against Shaun's side in her usual position. "Daddy?"

Jacobs lifted his glass at Shaun. "Nice to see that not all you young'uns are hoodlums and miscreants. Love to show you the place. You play golf?"

Oh boy. Chasing around a little white ball that had never done him any harm and beating it with a club. Exactly how he wanted to spend his days. *Not.* He took in a deep breath, and Gem's scent filled his head.

That's why he was doing this.

He smiled politely at her father. "No, sir, I don't, but I'm game for poker."

The colonel's brow rose. "We'll see about introducing you down at the club, but I doubt we'll have time to do it all while you're visiting. I can't imagine it'll take Gem that long to pack."

*Pack?*

Gem tugged him. "Oh dear, look at the time. We need to go—"

"Pack?" Shaun tilted his head at his father-in-law, wolf-style. "Why does Gem need to pack?"

The old man grumbled for a moment. "To get her things together to move up here to be with you. Since she told me that's what she's going to do."

Gem stopped pulling. Shaun's grin grew wider by the second.

"Oh, *that* reason for packing. How could I forget? Yes, we'll only be down south for... How long did you say, love?"

He turned and batted his lashes at Gem. She answered sheepishly. "Three weeks. Isn't that what we had talked about?"

"Of course. Silly me." He nodded at Mr. Jacobs. This conversation was finishing elsewhere. "Excuse us, sir, things to organize."

"No problem, I'll be here with the boys. We're going to a cancan show later."

Shaun tugged Gem by the arm and ducked into Evan's office. Privacy, now, was required. He let his happiness show as he leered at her.

"I'm not even going to mention the fact you made plans without me."

She lowered her chin, but maintained eye contact. "Tell me you're disappointed I want to live in the north. Go on, tell me,

245

so I can call you a liar."

His heart pumped like a jackrabbit in the midst of pursuit. "I can't support you the same way that you'd be living at home. I'm willing to make some changes in career, so I'm not off flying as often—but once you've got your degree, I bet you can get a position with any of the environment groups here in the north. They'd love to have someone with your enthusiasm and background."

Gem nodded. "I'm not too worried about finding work, Shaun. My hesitation has been trying to figure out where I belong. I like being with you, and I like trying new things. I loved running in my wolf, and I don't ever want to give that up."

*Thank God.* "I'm serious though, we can go south if you want to."

Gem smacked him on the chest. "What part of 'I like the north' did you not understand? There's a lot here for me to experience. I'm sorry I pulled a fast one on you with my father, but I decided it was easier to simply let him know what I wanted."

She snuck into his arms, and he held on tight. "Don't think I'm going to be too upset about you going around me, not when it means I get to keep the two things I love the most."

Shaun lifted her chin and kissed her again, the deep layers of having a mate settling around him and filling him with contentment. She was there for him, she encouraged him. Didn't seem to mind his rough edges.

Enjoyed spending time with him in the outdoors—he was in wolf heaven.

The kissing got a little rougher as she grabbed him by the jean pockets and tugged him closer. Just as it got real interesting, there was a knock on the door.

"Go away," Gem growled.

Shaun laughed. "Gem, this is Evan's office."

She rested her forehead on his chest. "Shoot. Forgot about that part."

He opened the door to discover Evan leaning against the doorpost. "May I come in?"

Shaun gestured to him magnanimously.

Gem had smoothed her skirt and stood politely to the side of the couch. "Sorry, Evan. I was a little distracted."

The Alpha shrugged. "Changes in circumstances can do that to you. Congrats, I heard you're planning on making the move permanent?"

She nodded. "If that's okay with you."

Evan dropped into his recliner. "Maybe."

Shaun kicked Evan's foot. "Maybe? What kind of bullshit answer is that?"

There was a pause as Evan tilted his chair back. "I just want to make sure I've got the whole situation in the right light. You moving to Whitehorse permanently means you're either in my territory and pack, or you're in the Miles Canyon pack. Shaun is strong enough to be Alpha if he wanted to. Am I looking at needing to fight the two of you in the next couple years?"

Shaun couldn't believe the turn in this conversation. "Why the hell would I want to take over the pack?"

"Because once you see something that needs to be done, with Gem chatting you up, you're going to find that you're doing the right thing all the time and suddenly it'll be work, work, work for me to keep control of you."

Gem laughed. "You're pulling our leg. You don't really think we're going to take over the Takhini pack, do you?"

Evan smiled broadly. "Actually, I was kind of hoping you'd

become Betas for the pack. Saves us fighting and all that."

It was like a curtain lifted. Somehow Shaun had known this was coming. "Betas? For Takhini?"

Evan shook his head. "You have this issue of repeating everything I say. I'm using small words, Shaun. You want to help lead or not?"

Shaun stared across to where Gem leaned on the back of the couch. She had a secretive little smile on her face, and he paused. Holy shit. "You knew. You knew about this too, and you didn't tell me?"

Gem shrugged. "Caroline approached me earlier. She wanted to be sure I was okay with a human being a part of the pack."

Damn, he was the last to learn anything. Still, ego aside for a minute— "Do you want this? You've given up your home in the south for me, do you really mean to give up your personal freedom and help run the insanity?"

"There's a difference between not having something because it's taken from you and offering to give it up. Huge difference."

"Yes or no, love?"

Gem nodded. "I think it would be a lot of fun to try as new experience."

Shaun shrugged. "Can't be worse than hanging out with Evan like I used to."

They grinned at each other. Shaun wanted to race over and pick her up, carry her all caveman-like down the hall to one of the back bedrooms. His wolf approved of both ideas. Damn thing was already preening from being given the Beta slot.

Evan rocked forward and shot to his feet.

"Drinks all around to celebrate." He hung his head out the

door and hollered. "Caroline, bring in the hootch. They said yes."

A loud cheer poured in the open door, and Shaun rolled his eyes. "The pack knew? Fuck it, Evan, everyone in the pack knew before me?"

Caroline walked in and winked at him, the moonshine in one hand and a glass of white wine in the other. "A few of them were taking bets how long it would be before you figured it out."

*Sheesh.* "Nice. Nice to know I'm starting with them all shaking in their boots over my mighty authority."

Caroline handed Gem the wine then passed Evan the bottle. "You're not the one they want to impress. They're hoping Gem thinks they're special."

Oh, they did, did they? Shaun sauntered over beside the couch and faked a menacing glare as he stared into Gem's eyes. "I know she's something special, and that's more than enough, right?"

Gem winked at him. "Right."

Shaun sat next to her, the girls continuing to chat. Evan passed him a tiny glass of something that smelled familiar.

His wolf twitched.

Shaun raised his glass as Evan proposed a toast. "To the Takhini pack's new Betas. May you find happiness in serving the whole crazy lot."

The instant the glass touched his lips, something tight wrapped around his throat. A loud cry of surprise rose from Gem, and Shaun whirled. He fell to the floor, trapped in his clothes.

He'd shifted to wolf without meaning to and the tight collar of his T-shirt was choking him.

"Shaun? What happened?"

He tugged on the clothing awkwardly with his wolf teeth as Gem attempted to help him, Evan laughing mercilessly in the background.

*"I'm not sure, I've never had that happen before."*

"You shifted when we first met, remember?"

Dangerous territory. Here be monsters. *"Umm, frankly, no, but I'll explain about that later..."*

Shaun took control of himself and shifted back, his shirt tangled around his head, the rest of his clothing a mess.

By now Caroline was giggling as well.

"Sure, laugh at the sickie. What the hell is up?"

It took a couple minutes to get himself back together. Gem very sweetly refrained from laughing. He picked up the shot glass from the ground.

"Sorry about the mess."

Evan shrugged and reached forward with the bottle again.

Shaun's belly quivered and his wolf howled in dismay. The world spun again.

"Shaun? Holy shit." Evan pulled the moonshine away, and Shaun stared up at his Alpha from his haunches, back in wolf form.

*"This is getting really boring, really fast,"* he complained to Gem.

Evan sat uneasily, shaking his head from side to side. "Oh man, I don't believe it. Sorry, dude, but I think I know the cause of your problem."

For the second time in less than five minutes, Shaun adjusted his T-shirt over his human chest. "Tell me, because flashing to wolf while I'm at twenty thousand feet could be more than awkward."

Evan placed the moonshine bottle on the side table away from Shaun then pointed at it. "You must be having a reaction to this."

*Shit, no.* "To your hootch?"

Evan nodded. "It's not your typical Jack and Coke. I'm not saying you can't drink, just not my special family blend. Your wolf is trying to stop you from getting looped again."

"A reaction, eh? That would explain why I had that hangover." Among other issues. Gem was giving him this very concentrated stare, and he wondered how much it would hurt when she found out about his little memory faux pas. He really needed to tell her the whole story as soon as possible.

His Alpha looked apologetic. "Sorry, man. I had no idea. It's not that common a reaction, but looks as if you won't be swilling the 'shine with me anymore."

"No, I don't think he will either." The precise princess tone in his mate's voice snapped Shaun's attention to her face.

The uber-polite smile she wore was...kinda scary. He swallowed hard. "Gem?"

She batted her lashes a couple times before delicately laying a hand on his arm. "Darling. So. You have no memory of shifting to a wolf the night we met? But you remember everything else, don't you?"

*Oh boy.* Damn those gods of karma—*as soon as possible* didn't mean right here, right now. Caroline suddenly got very busy doing something, but Evan happily stared, his gaze darting back and forth between Gem and Shaun as if he was watching a Wimbledon tennis match. Shaun wondered if having an audience was safer than dragging her from the room to complete his confession.

He motioned with his head for Evan to turn away. His Alpha shrugged as if confused, but his smile got wider. *Asshole.*

So be it. Time to man up—or wolf up. Whatever.

"No. I don't remember anything between talking with Evan—"

"—and drinking my hootch," Evan cut in.

Shaun squeezed the bridge of his nose. What a great thing, having a helpful friend in an already tough situation. "Yes, and I was drinking *his* hootch. The next bit I remember is waking up with you in the morning."

Gem patted his arm gently. "That must have been simply terrible for you."

The softer her voice, the more frightened he got. "It was. Wait...I mean it wasn't. I mean, I loved finding out we were mates, at least once we got past the fighting bit, and I have treasured every touch and every minute since... Oh shit." The longer he spoke, the higher her right brow rose. So much for sweet-talk—this conversation had gone south faster than an out-of-control tailspin. He cupped her face in his hands. "I was going to tell you, but..."

Faint music drifted through the shut door. Everything else went absolutely still as Shaun scrambled to find the best way to beg for forgiveness.

Evan's loud burst of laughter cut the silence. "Shaun, you mean you can't recall your first kiss with Gem? That's terrible. I remember kissing her in perfect detail."

This time both Gem and Shaun stiffened. Shock rolled through him as he watched her eyes widen. "You...you kissed Evan?"

Evan shot to his feet. "Oh dear, cat's out of the bag. Caroline, maybe we should—"

Shaun flung out a hand. "Whoa, puppy. You aren't going anywhere. You kissed my mate and you didn't tell me?" He turned to Gem in consternation. "You kissed him and never said a word?"

She gave him a dirty look. "You're really going to give me heck for not sharing that tidbit of information when you can't remember the first time we made love?"

Good point. Backing down immediately seemed vital to his continued health and happiness. "Right, you're right. I mean, it was only a kiss, and not anything else, but I'm still surprised..."

He stopped, distracted by Gem's reaction. She had flushed red, her mouth opening wide before she slammed her lips together.

Evan snorted.

Shaun spun to give his friend the evil eye. "What else did you do to her, you bastard?"

Caroline snickered in the background, and when all three of them pivoted to face her, she raised her hands in protest. "Sorry, just reacting to the sheer wolfishness of the moment. Let me summarize. Evan kissed Gem, Gem mated with Shaun, Shaun can't drink Evan's hootch. Sounds about typical for a day with the Takhini pack. You guys want to return to celebrating becoming Betas?"

Evan lifted his glass in the air in agreement before tossing the evil liquid back. Shaun discovered Gem nestling herself tight to his side. She smiled up at him as she tangled her fingers in his hair. Her lips twitched with amusement as she spoke quietly. "I think we can leave the rest of this discussion for later, don't you agree?"

*"You're going to kick my butt, aren't you?"*

The innocent delight in her eyes said more about forgiveness than pain coming his direction. *"Most definitely. But we can do it in private. Don't you think you deserve to grovel for a while?"*

Shaun breathed a sigh of relief. Groveling in private could be enjoyable. He'd have no problems letting her chastise him for his mistake in keeping secrets too long. Hmmm...punishment. *"I definitely deserve whatever you want to hand out. You should make it real official and dress-up for the occasion. Any chance you have thigh-high five-inch-heeled leather boots and a whip somewhere in your luggage?"*

Her eyes nearly popped out of her head. "Shaun!"

He grinned. Oh yeah. Apologizing was going to be a ton of fun.

Shaun led her back to the couch and tugged her halfway into his lap. The light brush of her lips across his cheek reassured him as he turned to speak to Evan. "So...where's the rule book for being Betas? My mate and I have to check to see what regulations we can break first."

Gem leaned against his chest and sighed, her fingers curled around his thigh. Something caught his eye, and he laughed as he lifted her hand into the air.

"You have pink nails."

The bright flash of her smile warmed him more than any hootch ever could. "And toes. I found this great little shop downtown that does fabulous manicures and pedicures. I have a standing appointment every week."

Caroline and Gem high-fived each other, and Shaun stared across the room at Evan. A deep sense of family rolled over him with a satisfying thud. Maybe this wasn't what he'd been looking for, but in the end? All of it was exactly what he needed. The pack, his mate.

In spite of looming bear wars, an overzealous father-in-law and more responsibility than ever before—his life was damn near perfect.

# About the Author

Vivian Arend has hiked, biked, skied and paddled her way around most of North America and parts of Europe. Throughout all the wandering in the wilderness, stories have been planted and they are bursting out in vivid colour. Paranormal, twisted fairytales, red-hot contemporaries—the genres are all over.

Between times of living with no running water, she home schools her teenaged children and tries to keep up with her husband—the instigator of most of the wilderness adventures.

She loves to hear from readers: vivarend@gmail.com. You can also drop by www.vivianarend.com for more information on what is coming next.

# SAMHAIN
### PUBLISHING

*It's all about the story...*

# Romance

# HORROR

www.samhainpublishing.com

CPSIA information can be obtained at www.ICGtesting.com
Printed in the USA
LVOW091534050712

288895LV00005B/27/P